Dare Me Tonight

CARLY PHILLIPS

One virgin, one night, one surprise baby…

For Ethan Knight, managing his empire is his priority. Women, not so much. But when a favor leads to him meeting sexy, driven Sienna Dare at a black tie corporate event, his interest is piqued along with his desire, and his infamous control slips as he joins her for an unforgettable night in bed.

Sienna Dare is trying to figure out the direction of her life when she meets enigmatic Ethan Knight—a strong, confident man so hot and irresistible he's the one she finally relinquishes her v-card to.

The problem? Ethan has a billion dollar contract with Sienna's brother at stake. An overly-protective brother who doesn't take it well when he finds out his business associate bedded his much younger sister. Oh, and she's pregnant, too . . .

Chapter One

S IENNA DARE WALKED into her half brother Ian's office in the Miami Thunder Stadium, still in awe of the fact that she had any kind of relationship with Ian at all, given their crazy dynamic. It had taken him years to accept her part of the family in his life, considering Sienna's mom had been their father's mistress. In true soap opera tradition, Robert Dare had two families. But they'd been working on making their peace as adults, and here they were now.

Considering how much she needed Ian's advice on her future, Sienna was grateful. She'd normally ask her older brothers for help, but Alex was away with his wife, Madison, on a business trip, and Jason was in New York City, running his nightclubs.

Her parents? Her father hadn't been around much lately, and her mother seemed wrapped up in whatever drama followed her father now. Sienna refused to think much about her parents' personal lives. She had enough to worry about on her own.

She knocked on the door, and knowing Ian was

expecting her, she stepped inside.

"What the hell did you do to your hair?"

She'd barely had a foot in the door when Ian raised his voice. And to think, she'd wondered if he'd even notice the change.

"Don't you like it?" She pulled on the long ponytail, grinning at the dark strands she saw in her peripheral vision.

Ian scowled. "You were blonde last time I saw you."

"And now I'm not. I dyed it." She sat down on the couch across the room from his desk, not put off by his typical bluster.

Maybe when she'd first met Ian, he'd frightened her with his gruff exterior, but she'd seen him with his sisters – his full-blooded sisters, Olivia and Avery – and knew there was a heart beneath the brusqueness. And lately, he'd extended that… she wouldn't call it sweetness… more like caring to her, as well. It helped that Alex worked for Ian at the Thunder team. The family was coming together. Considering *she* was the reason they'd been torn apart, the rapprochement made Sienna happy.

Ian was still frowning at her dark hair.

"Well, I like it," she informed him. "It's part of me finding myself," she said, not willing to be steamrolled.

He pushed himself to a standing position, looking

imposing as ever in his suit and tie, and walked over, joining her on the couch. "Look, I understand you graduated college and you're confused about what to do with your life."

She swallowed hard. "You can say that again. I'm twenty-three years old. I lost a year of school when I was sick, so I'm really old enough that I ought to know what I want. But I don't."

He tapped a pen on the table in front of him. "You have good choices ahead of you though. You're an extremely bright woman. You graduated summa cum laude in management and business, and you have an offer for a full scholarship to attend Columbia's exclusive Digital Business Strategy program. And I happen to know you've received an invitation to attend their NYC Weekend Scholars' Social starting this Saturday."

She raised an eyebrow at her half brother. "I can see why Avery says you know all and see all." She'd been avoiding RSVP'ing to the weekend event and she'd let the due date to reply lapse because she'd known then she'd have to make a decision on the program.

He shrugged. "I make it my business to know about my family and those I care about." He lowered his voice as he said, "You've become one of those people, Sienna."

3

She shifted uncomfortably. "Because I was the sick one? The baby with childhood leukemia?" She'd been in remission since she was seven thanks to the generosity of Avery's bone marrow donation.

Her dad, Robert Dare, had gone to his legitimate family, told them about his mistress and family on the side, blown their worlds and his marriage sky-high, and asked the kids to be tested to save Sienna. Her mother had known about the other wife and family all along. The kids had learned when the fallout happened. Not so for Ian and his side of the family.

"No, not because you were once sick," Ian said with a definitive shake of his head. "Because you're you and you've been nothing but good and kind to my siblings. And to me even when I was a jerk." His lips twitched, as much of a smile as Ian Dare gave. "So about the weekend in New York. I think you should go. It will give you good perspective on what to expect from the school and an idea about whether you'd like living in Manhattan."

She pulled her bottom lip between her teeth. "I, umm, let the RSVP lapse."

He rolled his broad shoulders, dismissing her concern. "And I took care of that for you. I told the school you'd be coming and I did you one better. I called an acquaintance of mine who is going to be your escort for the weekend."

"Ian!" He was so presumptuous and pushy. But wasn't that why she was here? So he'd help her make decisions?

"The school would have assigned you to someone anyway. This way you get someone I trust. Ethan Knight's company gives major donations to the school and to this program in particular," he went on, ignoring her outburst. "He'll take you to the formal the first night and give you an upscale tour of Manhattan the next day. By the time you leave, you'll have a good idea of whether the program is right for you. No pressure. And I know you'll be in good hands," he said, sounding very pleased with himself.

She sighed. She'd grown used to Ian's dominating personality. All the Dare siblings had, legitimate and illegitimate alike. "Fine. But can I get a flight to New York this late in the week?" Today was Thursday. She'd have to be there on Saturday.

"The corporate jet is fueled and ready for you. Any other concerns?" Ian asked.

A broad smile pulled at her lips. Now that he'd laid it out for her so simply, the weekend seemed more like an adventure than a chore or something that would make her feel coerced.

"I suppose I ought to go pack!" She bounced up from her seat, suddenly eager to check out Manhattan and experience this weekend, starting with the private jet. Her father, the hotel magnate, didn't fly them that way despite his wealth.

Sienna was all about new experiences. She supposed it had to do with nearly losing her life at such a young age. Although making permanent decisions about her future felt overwhelming, the easy things, like changing her hair, which she knew what it was like to lose, or going to check out New York City by herself, were exciting.

And she was looking forward to meeting the donor who would be her escort for the weekend.

ETHAN KNIGHT NEEDED a break. Hell, after the year he'd had, he deserved one. But as luck would have it lately, shit was piling up in every way.

His billion-dollar project for the Miami Thunder Football Stadium was a pain in the ass. The schematics for the deliverables had changed several times, and if a situation could go wrong, it did. His company, Knight Time Technology, KTT for short, supplied high-tech security for smart buildings and state-of-the-art corporate parks, and now, thanks to Ian Dare, a brand-new stadium. If they nailed this project, many more sports complexes and technology projects could come their way.

Needless to say, keeping Ian Dare happy had become a full-time job. The man was as hands-on as Ethan. Two demanding CEOs and Ethan had to do his best to accommodate the other man, not butt heads with him.

"What's up?" Sebastian, Ethan's brother, who also worked for KTT, asked.

"You wouldn't believe it if I told you." Ethan strode to the window in his office overlooking Manhattan and groaned.

"Try me," his youngest brother said.

Ethan shrugged. "Ian Dare's youngest sister is coming to New York this weekend. You know the Weekend Scholars' Social that Columbia hosts and we send a representative to in order to induce the brightest to attend their business school?"

"So we can hire them after? Sure do. I used to be the guy who attended on the company's behalf, remember? I was more than happy to turn that job over to people on our management team."

Sebastian shuddered at the memory, which didn't do much to make Ethan feel better about the upcoming event.

"Ian wants me to escort her personally," Ethan said.

Sebastian burst out laughing. "Oh, that's rich. Mr. Antisocial is going to make small talk with a graduate student-to-be."

Ethan turned around and faced Sebastian, leaning against the window, annoyed by his brother's obvious amusement at Ethan's expense. "She's twenty-three, almost twenty-four according to Ian. Not that much of a child." Just enough to get on his nerves with chatter, compared to his ripe old age of thirty-one. Lord knew, after all he'd been through, he felt ancient.

Still smirking, Sebastian said, "Maybe it'll be good for you. You know, get you out of the apartment and mingling with actual human beings. People who aren't family or minions that you can't yell at all the time?"

"Wiseass." Ethan ran a hand through his overly long hair.

"Well, the Thunder Stadium is priority one, so make sure you show this woman a good time. Smile a little. Maybe cut your hair?" Sebastian cocked an eyebrow.

Ethan scowled, annoyed. His brothers had been giving him shit about the length of his hair for a while now. Almost a year, to be precise. He used to be so meticulous, suits and ties pressed just so, hair cut every month by a ridiculously expensive guy at a salon, and he thought he was pleasing his wife.

Well, considering the wife had died of a self-induced accidental drug overdose and had also been undermining and stealing from his company, working with a supplier on a huge project to use substandard material and pocket the difference so she could support her drug habit, Ethan figured it was time for a lot of changes.

He was no longer going to twist himself inside out for a woman who wouldn't appreciate anything he did or gave to her anyway. Been there, done that.

He'd get through this weekend and go back to his happy hermit life.

✧   ✧   ✧

SIENNA LOVED THE private jet experience, felt like a princess for the two-and-a-half-hour flight, and now she was ready to take on Manhattan. She strode through the airport, looking for a sign with her last name on it. Ian had given her the name of her companion, Ethan Knight, and had assured her the man would be here himself to pick her up.

When she finally caught sight of her last name on a placard, a woman was holding up the card. With a shrug, Sienna headed toward the pretty female with light brown hair and blonde highlights, wearing a summer floral dress and shoes Sienna envied.

As she approached, Sienna waved. "Hi," she said, coming to a stop. "I'm Sienna Dare."

The woman flashed a genuine smile. "Nice to meet you. I'm Sierra Hammond, Ethan's sister. I'm so sorry he couldn't be here himself but there was an emergency at the office." Tucking the sign under her arm, she extended her hand, which Sienna shook.

"Sienna and Sierra. Cute," Sienna said, laughing.

The other woman chuckled. "I noticed the similarities, too."

"Thank you for picking me up."

"My brother really wanted to be here," Sierra said, obviously trying to reassure her.

Sienna waved away the woman's concerns. "I'm fine. Really." Sienna wasn't insulted in the least. If Ethan Knight was anything like Ian, he wouldn't have the time to be on airport duty.

Sierra seemed to relax at Sienna's easy attitude. "Okay, good. Well, I thought I'd take you to the apartment where you'll be staying and show you around. Do you need to wait for luggage?"

"No. I fit everything into my carry on." Sienna smiled brightly. "We're not going to a hotel?"

"No, my family owns a building on the Upper East Side of Manhattan. We have an apartment for out-of-town guests and Ethan thought you'd be more comfortable there."

"Sounds good."

They chatted on the limousine ride to the apartment. Sierra sat in the back beside Sienna, the driver knowing where to take them. Sienna discovered that Sierra was married to her longtime love, Ryder Hammond, with a baby girl at home. She also ran the Social Media Division at Knight Time Technology.

Listening to how the twenty-five-year-old woman had her life together made Sienna feel wistful that she wasn't anywhere near doing the same. But that was what this weekend was about, she reminded herself, trying not to feel too bad about herself. She had time to figure it all out.

She was led into a gorgeous apartment that was well decorated, with dark wood furniture and a leather sofa in the family room. She rolled her suitcase into the spacious entry area and set it off to the side.

"So this is it," Sierra said. "The bedroom is that door over there." She pointed to a back corner with a closed door. "The refrigerator is stocked, but anything you need, I want you to feel comfortable calling me."

They exchanged numbers, programming them into their phones.

"There's an itinerary on the table in the family room, but there will be a limo picking you up tonight for the gala, and my brother will be meeting you there. I promise," Sierra reassured her with a smile.

"No worries. It's all good."

Sierra hesitated. "I hate to just leave you, but I need to get home. We just wanted someone from the family to pick you up and make you feel comfortable, but if you need a tour guide for the afternoon…"

With a shake of her head, Sienna calmed the other woman. "I think I'll head over to one of the department stores and have my makeup done for tonight," she said, the idea popping into her head. And since she'd taken an early-morning flight, Sienna had the entire afternoon free. "I'm really used to being on my own. I'm fine."

"Oh, makeup sounds like fun. I wish I could join you. Do you want to get your hair done, too? Have the whole experience? My stylist is a friend. I'm sure he could fit you in?" Sierra offered. "Not that I'm saying you need your hair done." She sounded horrified at her choice of words.

Sienna burst out laughing. She really liked Sierra Hammond. "As a matter of fact, I would love to have my hair done for tonight."

Sierra pulled out her phone and dialed the salon, arranged a time, and ended the call. "All set. I'll text you the information. The car is at your disposal–"

Sienna shook her head. "I can take an Uber or a taxi, honest. It'll be fun to explore the city that way.

"No can do." Sierra shifted her purse higher on her shoulder. "I promised Ethan I'd take good care of you and that means the full chauffeured deal. Enjoy your time in New York," she said, starting for the door.

Before leaving, she turned back around. "Umm …

about my brother."

"Yes?"

"He can be…" She drew a breath and paused, as if hesitating about what to say. Finally she settled on a word. "Abrasive on a good day." She winced at her own choice. "I mean–"

"Don't worry. Ian Dare is my half brother. I know how to deal with gruff, uptight men."

"I hope you do," Sierra said before shooting Sienna a hopeful smile and walking out, shutting the door behind her.

✧   ✧   ✧

SIENNA HAD A fantastic afternoon getting herself made up for the night's event. Not only did she splurge, purchasing a ton of makeup and skin-care products after having her face done up at Saks Fifth Avenue, she left the salon with her newly dyed hair now blow-dried and curled.

She called Jason and talked him into meeting her for coffee because she was in town and when else could she see him? He seemed subdued, which was par for the course with her sibling, his life having taken an unexpected turn back in his college days. One event had changed and marked him forever. But she'd made him smile and she called that a win.

Then she took the limo back to the apartment and

headed upstairs with a bounce in her step.

Excited, she decided to call Avery and show her the end results of her day. After dumping all the bags on the bed, she pulled out her phone and Facetimed her half sister, who had, over the years, become one of her closest friends. Maybe all the Dares weren't BFFs, but the girls had definitely bridged the gap their father had created.

After the call rang a few times, Avery's face appeared on the screen. "Hi! How's New York?" she asked.

"Amazing. I pampered myself. Look." Sienna grinned into the camera phone and blew her a kiss, showing off her red lipstick.

"Oh, gorgeous!" Avery, a video blogger and married to one of the biggest rock stars in the world, Grey Kingston, lead guitarist and songwriter for the band Tangled Royal, knew a good makeover when she saw one. "And I really love your hair so dark. It makes your eyes pop!"

Sienna rolled her eyes. "I don't have those violet eyes of yours. Mine are crappy brown."

"Hot chocolate colored," Avery argued. "Now let me see your dress for tonight."

Sienna had hung up the outfit before she'd gone out earlier and she'd brought a travel steamer with her just in case the garment wrinkled. From the closet, she

14

pulled out the little black dress that flared out at the waist and held it up in front of her, showing it off for Avery.

"Ooh, the white piping makes the dress," Avery said, whistling her approval. "Shoes?"

"Mom lent me her black Louboutins." Sienna was more of a down-to-earth girl, but once in a while, dressing up was nice, and her mother's closet was full of fun, luxurious things. She held up the red-soled shoes.

"Nice!" Avery exclaimed.

Sienna and Avery didn't discuss their moms much, that being the one conversation that remained awkward. No matter how she looked at it, Sienna's mom, Savannah, had been Robert Dare's mistress/other woman with another family, while Avery's mom, Emma, had been in the dark. The good news was that Emma had remarried a nice man the family approved of, and that helped everyone get over the past.

"Do you know who you're meeting tonight?" Avery asked.

Sienna placed the dress and shoes on the bed and faced the phone again. "Ethan Knight, CEO of Knight Time Technology. The company is doing the tech and security for Ian's new stadium.

"Have you Googled him?" Avery met her gaze, then disappeared from the screen, leaving it blank, and

Sienna knew her sister was already busy on the browser. "Holy shit, he's hot!" she said, her voice coming through the phone.

"Show me. I need to know who to look for tonight."

Avery screenshotted a photo and sent it over Messenger. As soon as Sienna received the picture, she pulled up the photo and sucked in a startled breath.

Sienna had expected a stuffy older man who it would be difficult to spend the weekend with and pay attention to, not a sexy, gorgeous guy. Ethan Knight had dark short hair, with a handsome, freshly shaven face. In his suit and tie, he was the epitome of a CEO in charge of everything and everyone around him.

If not for the fact that she found him hot, she would have said his steely-eyed stare reminded her of Ian's. Although he was obviously older than her, he was by no means *old*, and he stirred something very primal in Sienna, something she'd never experienced before.

"Well?" Avery demanded.

"He's so good-looking," she whispered, unable to tear her gaze from the picture, those blue eyes startling and seemingly focused on her.

Avery laughed. "Someone is going to have a very good weekend."

"Hey, sugar, are you home?" Grey Kingston's distinct voice sounded from the other room.

"In the bedroom!" Avery called out. "Okay, my evening's about to start." She looked at Sienna. "And you need to get dressed for your date!"

Feeling herself blush, Sienna shook her head. "It's not a date! It's a school event," she said as much to remind her sister as to cement the fact in her own mind.

"With a private escort." Avery glanced over her shoulder as Grey's familiar face popped onto the screen.

"Hi, Sienna."

"Hey, Grey. We were just hanging up."

He grinned. "Always good to see you. But I wouldn't mind some time with my wife." He kissed Avery's cheek, and knowing what probably came next, Sienna called out, "Bye!" and disconnected the call.

She stared at her clothing, hoping her dress was appropriate for tonight's event. She hadn't chosen something stifling and conservative because that wasn't who she was and the invitation had said semi-formal. But she hadn't picked something overly revealing, either. She wanted to come off suitable for the occasion.

With that thought in mind, she headed for the bathroom to wash up and dress for the evening, unable to get the image of her host for the night from her mind.

Chapter Two

WITHOUT BRAGGING, ETHAN knew he was a hot commodity at this event. Business owners and CEOs wanted to talk to him, either about his ventures or his investments. It was another reason he hadn't wanted to come. Handing off the babysitting duty every year was a no-brainer, and for a while, it had been amusing to send Sebastian. Ethan supposed this was Karma paying him back, forcing him to spend the night making small talk with people he had no patience for and watching over a young woman he had nothing in common with.

Nevertheless, he did his duty. He mingled, speaking to men he'd known for years, introducing himself to their protégés, most of them wide-eyed, nervous potential students dressed in semiformal wear, too conservative even for him. Three-piece suits and handkerchiefs weren't his thing. He'd grown less stuffy over the last year, the things that mattered to him not as important. Not since they'd been thrown back in his face, the time and effort he'd put into making his marriage work not worth anything in the end.

Which was also the reason he'd had to do some serious ducking of women CEOs who'd heard of his widowed status and assumed now that a year had gone by since his wife's untimely death, they could attempt to make a pass at him. He wasn't interested. Instead he focused on trying to find the young woman he was supposed to meet up with.

Always prepared, Ethan looked for the blonde beauty with porcelain skin he'd seen during his scoping of Sienna Dare's social media pages. Yes, he'd checked her out. No, he didn't regret it. Any school or potential employer would do the same. Just because she was a business associate's sister didn't mean he'd slack off in his due diligence.

During his unsuccessful search of the room, his gaze kept straying to a young woman alone at the bar with jet-black hair in a sexier dress than many of the other women were wearing. His wife had been a blonde, and he hadn't been intrigued by another female since finding out about her betrayal, yet looking at this appealing woman alerted him to the fact that certain body parts still worked.

Good to know.

Didn't make him interested, but he was glad he wasn't dead inside. With a frown, he went back to his hunt for his weekend obligation. He'd sent a car to pick up Sienna Dare, knowing how awkward it would be for their first meeting to be alone in the back of a stretch limousine.

He checked his watch. It was a quarter after the hour, fifteen minutes since this affair had begun.

Where was she?

He was a stickler for promptness and this bordered on rude. He strode over to the bar and ordered a club soda, determined to keep his wits about him tonight. No sooner had he leaned forward on one elbow and ordered than he felt the woman's gaze on his.

He turned and looked her in the eye. Her skin glowed even under the poor bar lighting, her brown eyes sparkling. The one thing missing tonight was name tags. Someone would have their ass handed to them later, he assumed. But for now he merely met her gaze and glanced away before giving the wrong signals, his body be damned. This wasn't the right time or place.

"Excuse me," she said, stepping closer.

Her soft, fragrant perfume went straight to his dick, and he curled his hand around the glass the bartender had handed him.

"I'm looking for someone and you sort of look like him," she said.

He doubted this was a lame pickup attempt, here of all places, so he trusted the question was genuine.

"Just who do I look like?" he asked, now curious.

"My escort for the weekend. Ethan Knight of Knight Time Technology? I did some Googling and the photos had his hair much shorter than yours but you do look similar." She glanced up at him with an inquiring gaze.

He blinked in shock. "You're Sienna–"

"Sienna Dare," she said with an engaging smile, the red lipstick enhancing her natural beauty. "I had a feeling I was right! You're Ethan Knight?" Her light laughter sprinkled above the din of heavy voices surrounding them.

"I did my research, too, and you had blonde hair in your photos online," he mused, taking in the differences now. The black hair suited her. She'd been a beautiful blonde, but she was a striking brunette.

"Surprise!" she said with an easy shrug. "I tend to grow bored and make changes." Her astute stare swept over him, focusing on his face. "So do you. Your hair is much longer than the one on the KTT website."

He admired the fact that she was diligent, looking into who she'd be meeting ahead of time, and he extended his hand.

She shook it.

He wasn't prepared for the tremor of awareness that reverberated up his arm and went straight to his cock. He blinked in shock. Her red lips parted in

surprise, letting him know she'd felt the sexual awareness between them, too.

Worse, as those luscious lips parted, all he wanted
was to feel that mouth wrapped around his now raging
erection. It'd been a year since he'd wanted sex, let
alone one particular woman. Why the hell did it have
to be this one? Ian Dare had sent her to Ethan to take
care of, not fuck. The man was also the most important client Ethan had had in a long time, and that
was saying something because all his clients represent-
ed multimillion- and billion-dollar deals.

Ian had made it a point of mentioning Sienna
wasn't going back to business school later in life, as
many tended to do. No, she was just shy of twenty-
four, which made her way too young for Ethan. Not
to mention the obvious wide-eyed innocence and
appreciation of the mundane that was the distinct
opposite of his jaded thirty-one years.

"Mr. Knight?" Her soft voice pulled at him and
she reached out, her hand touching his forearm.

Oh, fuck. "Ethan," he said on a low growl.

"Ethan," she said, clearly not put off by his gruff
demeanor. "I said it's nice to meet you and I appreciate you taking time out of your busy schedule to take
care of me this weekend."

"You're welcome," he said roughly. "I'm sorry I
didn't pick you up from the airport. I had an emergen-

cy and couldn't get away. I figured my sister would take good care of you." He didn't want her upset with him and reporting back to her brother that he'd bailed.

She waved away his concern, his gaze falling on the red nails that matched her lips. Jesus, was everything about her appealing?

"Honestly it was fine. Ian is a busy executive, too. I'm used to how things work, and I'm good with taking care of myself."

He relaxed on that score. Ian wasn't going to come after him for leaving some frightened girl alone in New York City. This woman knew how to take care of herself.

"So how are you enjoying your time in Manhattan?" he asked. He didn't want to hit her up with her school and career plans right away and scare her off. Ian had mentioned she was hesitant about going to graduate school, so he planned to ease into that part of the conversation.

"I love it!" Her eyes lit up at the question. "Since I had the afternoon free, I took advantage and enjoyed myself." She blushed and he wondered how she'd kept busy.

"What did you do with yourself?" He wasn't usually so talkative, but she was easy to be with.

"I don't want you to think I'm shallow. I'm here for a business school weekend," she murmured, intriguing him.

"How about if I promise not to judge you?"

She ducked her head, then said, "I went to Saks and had my makeup done, and your sister recommended her hairstylist and I had a full salon day."

He took in her gorgeous, expressive features, the makeup that defined her brown eyes, and the lips he wanted to devour and appreciated the effort she'd made. He would have liked to compliment her but knew how inappropriate anything he said would be, so he remained silent.

"But I'm not all about the frilly, girly stuff," she went on to assure him. "I'm honestly interested in your business and what kind of security you're doing at the stadium. I'd love to know more about why you feel this school is the right place for me and discuss my future," she said, clearly nervous about the fact that she'd revealed her more frivolous side.

As a normal rule, he wouldn't be interested in anything she'd had to say. He'd expected conversation to be forced and stilted, but he had a hunch this woman could discuss nail polish color and he'd be listening and drooling as she spoke.

He glanced at the open terrace, where people had congregated. "Let's go outside," he said, needing some fresh air that might dissipate her scent and its effect on his body.

"Sure. It's a beautiful night," she said, as he gestured for her to walk ahead of him.

Big mistake, he thought, his stare on her long legs and high heels that he imagined wrapping his hips while he fucked her.

So he lifted his gaze to her trim waist. She was thinner than the women he usually went for, her body more delicate, and yet that didn't stop him from imagining the things he could do as he pounded into her.

Yeah. This was a fucking bad situation. "So tell me about yourself," he said when they finally reached the balcony and he could breathe in the outside air, free of her scent.

"I graduated summa cum laude in management and business from Florida State University."

She rolled her shoulders as if it were no big deal. He knew for a fact just how hard she'd had to work to accomplish those things.

"I'm just tired of studying," she admitted, leaning in as if telling him a secret.

Too close and her fragrance was back in his nostrils, filling his body, making him harder. "But you have an offer for a full scholarship to attend Columbia's exclusive Digital Business Strategy program. It's elite, you know."

She blew out a breath from those lips. "I do.

Which is why I feel guilty considering turning it down. And I realize that no matter what business you're in, a big part of any strategy is digital. You want to be able to reach consumers and businesses online where they live and observe their behaviors and figure how to tap into their market." She sighed. "But I'd rather live it than learn it, if that makes any sense."

He admired that she understood things about herself most people struggled to discover. She was also clearly bright, something that everyone in this room could claim, but she was enchanting, as well.

"On the other hand," she went on, "if I want to succeed, I need the education."

"And do you want to succeed? In digital business strategy or anything like it?"

A secretive smile pulled at her lips as she placed both hands out and shrugged. "I'm unsure, Mr. Knight—"

"Ethan." He let out another little growl, not wanting the formal distance between them.

"Right. Ethan. Part of me just wants to dive in and just … *do*."

Far be it from him to push her to go to school when she wasn't sure what her path should be. "One thing I'm certain of, you'll put one hundred percent into whatever it is you choose to do. I can tell that from this one conversation alone." She was an excited ball of energy and drive but one without direction, he thought.

He'd like to direct that enthusiasm, he mused, thinking of her on her knees in front of him. He shook his head and refocused on the task at hand. Discussing the courses offered at Columbia, doing his job as someone who both funded and hired from this school.

But all the while, his mind kept drifting to Sienna Dare, not as a potential student or employee, but as the first woman who had interested him sexually in longer than he cared to remember. He had the distinct feeling she would be incredibly difficult to forget, and as the evening came to an end, he found himself reluctant to part from her, something he never could have anticipated.

It was everything about her, how she went from youthful free spirit to bright businesswoman capable of having a serious conversation about topics that would have most people's eyes glazing over. The way she spoke, so animated and excitedly, as if everything she said had great importance. She alone had taken him away from the burdens that consumed him day in and day out, making him forget everything but the joy of being with her.

He'd allowed her the freedom to talk to other trustees, donors, and CEOs who could enlighten her on the program and the benefits of furthering her education here, despite hating every second of her focus being on other people and not him.

At the moment, another man had captured her attention, an older gentleman who was clearly interested not just in what she had to say about social media marketing strategy, but was also inching nearer to her the longer they talked.

Ethan might not be much better than this man when it came to noticing Sienna's charms, but there was no way he was going to let the man monopolize her attention or behave inappropriately on his watch.

As the guy inched closer and Sienna took a visible step back, Ethan swooped in. "The night's about over and, Cooper, isn't your protégé waving, trying to get your attention?" As soon as the man glanced over his shoulder, Ethan hooked his arm into Sienna's and walked her away.

"Oh, thank goodness!" she said, laughing. "I thought he would never stop talking. And he was in my personal space and I hate when people don't get the hint that they're just standing too close." She shivered.

Ethan noticed she hadn't pulled away when he'd slid his arm into hers and begun walking her out of the room. He wasn't too close, nor did she dislike him in her personal space, and that thought pleased him greatly.

"Tonight went so quickly!" she said as they waited for the elevator. Nobody else was with them at the moment.

"Have you come to a decision?" he asked.

She sighed. "I'm afraid not."

"Well, there's still tomorrow. I'll show you around Manhattan and you can ask me any questions you still have about the Digital Business Strategy program."

She beamed up at him. "I would love that!"

"For now, though, I'll see you home."

She glanced at him, those brown eyes looking as if they could see right through him and read his ulterior motive – wanting to be with her longer. Something he was having a difficult time admitting even to himself.

"You already sent a car for me. I don't mind grabbing a taxi or an Uber," she assured him. "And don't worry. I won't tell Ian."

She grinned at her words, but Ethan was very aware of her brother as a factor in how he treated her. But as he looked at her, it was difficult to care much about Ian or the stadium contract at all. His body, his very being, seemed to reach out to hers with both desire and need.

"That won't be happening. I'll make sure you get home safely." He didn't think she was aware of the fact that he lived in the same building where she was staying, and for now he kept that to himself.

"Well, thank you. I appreciate that," she murmured.

As they stepped onto the street, Ethan immediately recognized his driver standing beside the limo, and Ethan nodded at Mason, who had been by his side for years.

He slid into the back seat beside Sienna, allowing himself to breathe in her delicious scent without berating himself for the indulgence. She couldn't see his throbbing erection in the darkness of the car, and she'd remain unaware of her effect on him.

After he walked her to the door and said good night, he'd just have to self-gratify to the thought of her perfect lips, sexy body, and smart brain. The entire package that was Sienna Dare turned him on beyond belief. He wasn't used to denying himself, but in this case he had no choice. There was nothing more he could do.

SIENNA SAT BESIDE Ethan Knight in the back seat of the darkened limo, a mess of nerves and desire. She wasn't used to feeling either. The man was the epitome of perfection, from the long hair she hadn't expected, to the light scruff on his face, to the casual way he wore his expensive suit, the white shirt unbuttoned just enough to tease her with his hint of chest hair peeking through. And the way he smelled? All man with a delicious hint of musk.

The guys she was used to from college were boys in comparison to Ethan Knight, and she more than felt the difference both in her body's reaction to him and in his response to her. Oh, he tried to keep a respectful distance, but she didn't miss the way his stare zeroed in on hers when she was with other people, how he watched her with interest in his gaze that had nothing to do with convincing her to attend business school in New York City.

She'd had enough half sisters fall in love for her to be well aware of what chemistry between two people was like. And she and Ethan had chemistry in spades.

Shocking sexual desire made her aware of her body for the first time, caused a slickness between her thighs and a yearning she wasn't going to find easily in men back home. Ethan was intelligent and aloof, qualities that didn't put her off because of the type of men in the family in which she'd grown up.

In the past, she'd dated, she'd made out with guys, but ultimately she'd kept her distance, at least from any significant relationships, and for good reason. Sienna's life had always been serious, from her childhood illness to her family drama, and though she didn't act or live in the shadows, she wanted someone who could handle everything that came along with her.

She knew better than to create fairy tales. Her parents' relationship had taught her that happily ever after came with strings. Sometimes with another family. So she'd waited for just the right person to be with. She leaned her head against the headrest and glanced at Ethan. A man, not a boy. The more she thought about school, the less likely it became that she'd accept. So one night with a guy she wanted beyond reason before she would head back to Miami, where she belonged?

Everything inside her screamed yes. Ethan was the right one.

She could handle the distance he attempted to put between them and was more than willing to try and breach it. She just needed to work up her nerve, and the charged silence between them in the car gave her time to think.

To plan.

The car pulled to a stop in front of the familiar building in which she was staying. To her surprise, Ethan climbed out first, then waited for her to join him.

She assumed he was saying good night, which meant she'd have to make her move.

"Are you ready to go up?" Ethan asked.

She blinked at him. If he planned on walking her to her door, she didn't have to attack him in the street, in front of the driver.

Her stomach was bouncing with nerves as he guided her into the building.

"Mr. Knight," the doorman said. "Welcome home."

"Thank you, John. Have a nice evening." He placed a hand on her back and guided her toward the elevators.

Sienna glanced up at him. "Home? Sierra mentioned your family owned the building, but she didn't say any of you lived here."

His grin was as surprising as it was infectious. "Penthouse," he explained, a man of few words, as usual.

They stepped into an open elevator, and he hit the second floor, where she was staying. A few seconds later, she was standing in front of her door, Ethan beside her.

He braced a hand above her head, leaning closer than would be appropriate for their supposed positions. She took it as a sign.

"I hope you enjoyed yourself," he said.

"The night was more than I hoped for." She spoke the truth. *He* was more than she'd hoped for. "You were an excellent host."

The silence between them was charged, her heart beating rapidly in her chest, possibilities soaring through her brain.

"Good night, Sienna." He spoke but he didn't leave.

She couldn't bring herself to use the key she'd taken out of her purse, either. She stared up at him, unable to break eye contact, and forced herself to utter the words she needed to say. "Please stay."

ETHAN HAD AN angel on one shoulder, a devil on the other. He knew what he should do. Angel. But he was too aware of what he wanted. Desired. Devil.

"This isn't a good idea," he said, their gazes mere inches apart.

"But it's what *you* want." Her tongue ran over those seductive lips.

Had he been obvious in his need? He thought he'd disguised his yearning well. Apparently not.

The desire in those brown eyes made it impossible to say no.

He needed a drink and he needed her. "Unlock the door."

With trembling hands, which reminded him of how innocent she was compared to him, she let them inside. He knew the layout of the apartment, was aware there was always alcohol stocked in the liquor cabinet.

Without speaking, he strode over and pulled out a

bottle of Macallan, pouring himself a drink, taking a stiff, long sip. He didn't offer her one even though she was more than old enough. If they were going to do this, she was going into it aware of her choices.

He turned to face her, her gorgeous eyes focused on him. Her lips, still red, parted slightly.

"One night and we tell no one," he said, maybe too harshly. But she needed to know the score.

A flash of what appeared to be pain flickered in her eyes before she nodded in agreement.

"Your brother would have my head on a platter," he muttered, finishing off the drink and pouring another. Ian had sent her to him for protection, not seduction.

But who was seducing whom? he asked himself. She'd asked him to come in. Excuses, he thought, flimsy and not worthy of him or her.

"Ian's my half brother and he won't hear a word from me," Sienna agreed.

He inclined his head, accepting her at her word.

He recalled hearing stories of the Dare family and the extreme scandal with multiple families, but the details eluded him now. He assumed whatever it was had to do with the fact that she and Ian weren't fully related. Somehow Ethan had a feeling Ian wouldn't think the distinction mattered if he discovered Ethan had fucked his sister. A multibillion-dollar contract was at stake, and Ethan still couldn't bring himself to care.

He wanted Sienna and he meant to have her.

✧　✧　✧

HOLY SHIT. SIENNA stared at the man she'd propositioned. She wasn't sure she'd really thought that he'd agree, and now that he had? She needed to gather her courage.

She reached down and pulled off one heel, then the other. "Umm, make yourself comfortable. I'll go change and be back," Sienna said and headed into her bedroom, closing the door behind her.

She tossed the shoes on the floor and leaned against the wood, forcing air into her lungs. What did she do now? Although she'd sworn not to say a word, she decided Girl Code overrode that promise, and she dialed Avery on her cell, whispering when the other woman answered.

"Avery?"

"Sienna? Are you okay? Why are you whispering?" Avery asked, whispering back.

"Who is it, sugar?" Grey's voice.

"Tell him it's me, I'm fine, and go into another room," Sienna instructed.

"Okay, I'm in the bathroom, door closed. What in God's name is going on?" Thank God Avery did as she was told.

"I found the guy. The one. He's in the other room now and I'm freaking out!" She didn't tell Avery who she was with. Her half sister and best friend would pick up on the pertinent details.

"Oh my God. You're going to lose your virginity!" Avery squealed.

"Shh! Just tell me I can do this. I need to know I'm not crazy."

Avery's breathing sounded over the phone, and then, "You waited this long. If you've found the guy, you've found the guy. Now pull up your big-girl thong and get back in there!" she instructed.

Laughing, which broke the tension and was just what Sienna needed in the face of Ethan's intensity, she relaxed, comfortable again with her decision. "I'm going. Thank you! Bye!"

She breathed out, brushed her teeth, and went to undo her dress only to find she couldn't reach the back herself. So that was how it was going to go.

She drew a steadying breath and returned to ask Ethan for help. She stepped back into the room.

He'd removed his jacket and hung it over a chair and rolled up the sleeves of his dress shirt, revealing tanned, muscled forearms.

She swallowed hard and, knowing she was blushing, said, "I need help with my dress."

His eyes darkened at the request, ice darkening to a darker, sexier shade of blue.

She turned, pulling her long hair to one side.

He placed his empty glass on the nearest table and strode over, all her senses aware of him as he came closer. His seductive scent, the heat of his body, the sharp inhale of his breath as he placed his big hands behind her and slowly, seductively pulled down the zipper, until she felt the rush of cool air on her bare back and the warmth of his breath near her neck.

She was more aware than ever of the tiny scrap of lace she called underwear and the matching bra she'd chosen to wear. Just because she'd liked the set, not because she'd ever thought anyone besides her would see it.

His breath hissed out, and suddenly his calloused finger traced a line down her spine, causing her nipples to peak and tighten with awareness, sharp spikes of desire shooting to her core.

He slid the sides of her dress down and the garment dropped to the floor, leaving her bared to him in more ways than just physical. She hadn't been prepared for such intensity, though she should have been. Everything about Ethan Knight was potent. Tonight had the power to change her world except, as he'd reminded her, it was one night.

A night never to be shared with anyone. She'd ignored the dagger she'd experienced at being relegated to his dirty secret, telling herself she understood. Sometimes there were reasons for discretion, and with everything at stake for him with the Miami Thunder Stadium, his request made perfect sense.

Even if it dug at the very pieces of her heart that she'd glued together over the years.

Tonight was about sex. Desire. A yearning so strong she was ready to give up the thing she'd held on to, waiting for the right time. The right man.

She'd found him, she thought, turning and finding herself in his arms, backed against the wall, his mouth coming down hard on hers.

Chapter Three

ETHAN KISSED SIENNA like a starving man, and that's what he was. A man deprived of human connection and affection for longer than he cared to remember. Everything about this woman called to his deepest primal instincts to take and possess. He didn't care what family she belonged to or how she could screw up his business, he just wanted her.

And she'd made the overture, which meant she was on board.

Her lips were soft, her body ready for him. He lifted her into his arms, her legs wrapping around his waist as he backed her against the wall. For as much as he desired her and wanted to lose himself inside her, he let himself indulge first in her taste, a minty sensation that let him know she must have brushed her teeth during her little bathroom escape.

He slid his tongue around her mouth, warming up the coolness so he could experience her flavor for himself. It was a hot kiss, one he got lost in until the soft moan that came from the back of her throat reverberated throughout his body.

He slid his fingers into her soft hair, curled his hand around the long strands, and tipped her head to the side, his mouth trailing from her lips to her neck, nuzzling the delicious skin there. She held on to his forearms, taking what he gave and finding his mouth again so she could return the kiss with equal fervor. Not passive, she began to pull at the lapels of his jacket, pushing them off his shoulders.

He slid her down the length of his body, feeling her soft suppleness arousing him. With shaking hands, she began to work at the buttons of his shirt until he couldn't stand the delay and ripped open the sides, sending the small studs scattering.

At the unexpected action, she sucked in a startled breath, then her gaze came to his chest and her eyes opened wide. She splayed her fingers across his skin, her smaller, pale hand resting where his heart beat rapidly for her alone. There didn't seem to be a need for words. Ethan wasn't a man of many to begin with, and she seemed more than content with his actions.

He grasped her wrist, bringing her hand up to his lips and pressing a hot, wet kiss against her skin, her pulse tapping out a furious beat.

He took in her sexy body, the skimpy lingerie that covered parts of her he was dying to see, and any restraint he'd been holding on to fled. He released the clasp of her bra, and as the garment fell away, her small but perfect breasts came into view. Unable to resist, he dipped his head and swiped his tongue over one nipple, licking, tasting, and teasing the tight bud, discovering her sweetness before she became too sensitive, trying to pull away.

So he switched to the other side, giving the other nipple the same torturous treatment. When she squirmed before him, he held her in place, his hands on her hips as he devoured her with his mouth. Only when she'd had enough did he release her and slip his hands into the sides of her panties, pushing them to the floor, kneeling as he removed the garment.

His nostrils filled with the scent of her sex, making him aware of how completely aroused she was. For him. His cock throbbed against the uncomfortable fabric confining him, and he knew it was time.

He scooped her into his arms and discovered she was a light little thing as he carried her through the living area and into the bedroom on the far side of the apartment. Already the room looked lived in with feminine pieces of clothing and items strewn around the bed. Ignoring them all, he placed her down on the center of the mattress and paused only to pull out his wallet and retrieve a condom his brother, Sebastian, had put there a few weeks ago along with the suggestion to go and get himself laid. Never would he have imagined he'd use it so soon.

From there, he removed his pants, yanking down his boxer briefs along with them, fully aware of her wide-eyed gaze on him the entire time. His cock sprang free, and as he crawled onto the bed, she reached out and wrapped her hand around the rigid length, moaning at the feel of him.

He jerked in her hand. "Jesus, I'm going to come just from you touching me," he muttered, the first words he'd spoken to her since this had begun.

"Yeah?" Eyes open and focused, she swiped her thumb over the pre-come on the head of his dick, and his own eyes nearly rolled back in his head.

She clearly wasn't practiced, but she didn't need to be when just the touch of her was enough to set him off.

He gritted his teeth and ripped open the condom, pinching the tip and rolling the protection over his aching shaft, her gaze watching his every move.

He settled between the inviting spread of her thighs. Grasping his cock, he held on as he glided himself over the bare lips of her slick sex. Beads of sweat broke out on his forehead, the need to be inside of her greater than anything he'd felt before. But something made him go slower, take his time with her, sliding his cock back and forth over her clit until she writhed beneath him, desire obviously pummeling at her as it was him.

He met her heavy-lidded gaze and something shifted between them. A moment that was quick yet impactful, heavy in its significance yet one that passed quickly. And then he was bracing one hand on the mattress, the other holding on to his cock as he breached her entrance and pushed inside.

She was hot and wet, so tight she strangled his dick with her inner walls, and he'd be lucky not to come in one thrust. As he pushed deeper, she clenched tighter, and he couldn't hold back the groan from the his throat.

"Jesus, you're so fucking tight it's almost like no man's ever fucked you before."

At his words, she sucked in a shocked breath.

His gaze flew to hers, and he saw the raw truth in her deep brown eyes.

"Son of a bitch. Seriously?" he asked, unable to grasp the fact and unwilling to face the importance of its meaning.

She gripped his forearms. "Don't stop."

Whether intentional or not, her insides clenched him tighter and he lost control. He couldn't halt if he wanted to. And fuck him, he didn't. He'd deal with the ramifications afterwards.

He held on to enough thought and care to slowly guide himself out and back in, her wetness easing his way as he glided into her, refraining from heavy thrusting only by the merest thread of sanity. Finally he was all the way in, balls deep in her slick body.

He glanced at her face and saw only awareness and need, and as she squeezed him tighter, pleasure crossed her pretty features. He allowed himself to let go and take her, pumping his hips in and out, grinding their bodies together each time they joined, fully aware of her soft sighs of pleasure that grew louder the faster he moved.

He thrust harder each time, and finally she cried out, her body convulsing in gratification as she came.

"Ethan!" She called out his name, triggering his climax, and he climaxed hard and long. His body not content with a quick release, he pumped into her over and over, needing more from her.

Wanting to hear his name on her lips again.

Reaching between them, he slid his fingertip over her clit, and she gasped. He pinched and she screamed, coming again, yelling his name as he spilled the last of himself inside her.

He collapsed on top of her, slowly coming to himself and becoming aware of her heavy breathing beneath him. Only then did the reality of the situation sink in. He hadn't just broken his dry spell, he'd done it with Ian Dare's fucking sister, a woman he had no business going anywhere near and a goddamned virgin to boot.

And for the moment, he couldn't bring himself to care.

Rolling over, he stood up from the bed and walked to the bathroom, disposing of the condom, then finding a washcloth and rinsing it under water. He returned to discover her waiting, looking up at him with an uncertain look on her face.

With care that was unlike him, he placed the cloth between her legs and cleaned her up, hoping like hell she wasn't sore and, if she was, that this would help.

When he was finished, he threw the washcloth on the floor and glanced at her. "Why didn't you tell me?"

She blinked at him. "Would you have gone through with it if you'd known?"

"Fuck no."

A pretty smile pulled at her lips. "There's your answer. I wanted you. You wanted me. And I wasn't about to deny us what we both desired."

He groaned. Fine. It was done. And it wasn't like it was some great Greek tragedy. She was an adult, capable of making her own decisions. He just had no intention of asking her why she'd chosen him for her first time. That road could only lead to disaster and messy emotions that had no place in a one-night stand.

He glanced at her satisfied expression and had not one ounce of regret. In fact, he couldn't say he was wholly satisfied yet and that thought took him by surprise.

He shrugged. He wasn't a literal man. One night didn't mean one time only, he mused. They'd just have to be creative since he'd used his one and only condom, and feeling her mouth around his cock was something he'd definitely want to experience.

He gestured for her to shift over so he could pull down the covers. And then, defying every rational thought that ran through his head, he climbed back into bed beside her and pulled her into his arms.

Because he wasn't yet finished with Sienna Dare.

SIENNA SIGHED IN utter pleasure in Ethan's arms. As first times went, she figured that was pretty damned good. She suppressed a giggle. After all, she was familiar with her vibrator, so it wasn't like she'd never had anything inside her before. She'd actually been shocked he'd realized it at all.

"What's so funny?" he asked, his voice a low growl beside her.

"I was just thinking that, for a first time, it was okay."

She immediately found herself flat on her back, Ethan's big body looming over her. "Just okay?" he asked on a growl she discovered turned her on. Big-time.

"Pretty good?"

The growl got lower, deeper, until she felt it pulsing in her core. "Excellent but I wouldn't mind a repeat?"

Her stomach chose that moment to growl, and it wasn't a small, ladylike noise, either. Her cheeks flushed in embarrassment.

"Did you eat anything at the event?" he asked.

She shook her head. She'd been too nervous beforehand and she'd basically ignored the offerings during the evening.

"Let's order in." He pulled out his phone and pulled up an app. "Pizza? Chinese?"

"You decide. You know what's good around here."

"Chinese."

A few seconds later, he'd ordered. "The place is around the corner and they show up in like ten minutes. I always wonder if they're just microwaving the stuff, but the food is really good." He stood up and pulled on his pants. She couldn't tear her gaze away from the happy trail of hair that led into the waistband or the abs above it.

The man was spectacularly built and her mouth watered at the sight of him. Now that she knew what it was like to have him inside her, she couldn't wait to do it again. Unfortunately, or fortunately for her stomach, he was right and the doorman called up before she could even process her thoughts.

They sat in the kitchen, her wearing a tee shirt and no underwear – because he wouldn't let her put them back on – and they ate delicious dumplings, spare ribs, and a whole host of other items he'd ordered for them. By the time she was finished, not only was she full, she was yawning.

"Go on in. I'll clean up and meet you inside," he said.

"Are you sure? I can help."

"I've got it."

Thrilled he wasn't rushing away from her, something she'd expected him to do the minute they'd finished having sex, she nodded and headed back into the bedroom and climbed into bed. While he cleaned, she heard his phone ring and him answer, taking the call, and though she hadn't meant to, she fell asleep to the low rumble of his voice and the sounds of him cleaning up in the other room.

SIENNA CAME AWAKE to the distinct feeling of arousal, a heavy, delicious rush of warmth traveling through her veins, a pulsing deep in her core, and the heat of Ethan's body pressed tight against her backside. Her nipples puckered to the caress of big hands wrapped around her breasts, fingertips pinching one of the tight buds until she squeezed her legs together and realized a hard male thigh was between them.

Still sleepy, she was more than aware of Ethan manipulating her body until his cock jutted between the lips of her sex and pushed inside her, filling her and making her whole.

She moaned at the delicious invasion, accepting him as he thrust into her from behind, his fingers still playing with her breasts, arousing her from both angles.

Now this was the way to wake up, she thought, as he began to slide in and out of her, the head of his cock hitting a particularly sensitive spot at this new angle.

"Oh God."

He pinched her nipples harder. "Come," he whispered in her ear, and to her shock, her body began to ripple around him, waves of sensation sending her up and over into bliss.

He began to thrust and take his own pleasure, when suddenly a curse spewed from his throat. "Fuck."

Next thing she knew, he jerked out of her and was coming on her back, jets of semen coating her in what felt like an erotic stream. He groaned through his release as she accepted the warm liquid on her skin.

"Shower," he said gruffly, and picked her up like she weighed nothing and carried her into the bathroom.

The shower was much like all of their interaction since he'd agreed to come into her apartment last night, quiet and intense, which pretty well described the man himself. This wasn't an affair, it was a night of sex, and he was treating it as such.

She couldn't say she minded, although the softer inside part of her wished he'd talk about himself. Tell her why he was so closed off and let her get to know him. Knowing that wasn't what she'd agreed to, she forced herself to enjoy the here and now, fully aware going forward that one-night stands and sex for the sake of sex weren't her cup of tea.

But she'd take every minute she could get with Ethan Knight before her plane took off later tonight.

ETHAN WASN'T, NOR had he ever been, a New York City sight-seeing kind of person. He didn't care about seeing the Statue of Liberty, the Empire State Building, or the new One World Trade/Freedom Tower downtown. But he had to admit, after giving Sienna the choice of what she'd like to do today, he was glad she'd decided on the more touristy activities than shopping on Fifth and Madison Avenues like Mandy would have done.

He still had a bitter taste in his mouth from the lifestyle his wife had led, both before and after her addiction came to light. And though he'd worked like a dog to give her everything she could have wanted in life, apparently it hadn't been enough. So the fact that Sienna preferred to learn about the town as opposed to spending her family's money gave her an edge, as far as he was concerned.

He was shocked to find he'd enjoyed the day, including the ferry ride to the Statue of Liberty. Watching her indulge in street cart vendors' huge pretzels and a hot dog for lunch, followed by a sad tour of the Freedom Tower, and ending with a pedicab ride back to the apartment, had been one of the more enjoyable afternoons he'd ever spent. Not that he'd admit as much to his siblings, who would never let him hear the end of it.

The time with Sienna had shown him what a bastard he'd been to the people around him lately, especially his family, who'd put up with his asshole tendencies. He'd let his anger over Mandy consume him, and though he couldn't say those emotions were gone, his time with Sienna had opened him up to his lighter side. One he'd missed.

During their walks, they'd talked about career possibilities for her, and though he'd touted the attributes of the program like a loyal donor, he got the distinct impression school wasn't on her agenda. He wondered how Ian would take the news. For Ethan, it meant she wouldn't be in Manhattan, and though this should make him happy – he did not need knowing she was in the same town as a distraction – he couldn't stop the nagging part of him that was disappointed by the notion.

And that meant it was a damned good thing she was leaving in an hour. He needed to know this girl was out of his system for good.

He waited in the living room while she packed up her bags, planning to escort her to the airport. She finally walked back inside, wearing jeans and a tee shirt, a sweater tied around her waist. She'd freshened up after their long day, but she didn't have any makeup on, giving her an even more youthful, beautiful look.

"Ready to go!" She pulled her carry-on along with her.

He cleared his throat. "The car is waiting downstairs."

Her lips turned into a cute little pout he wanted to kiss off her face. "I won't make the *I can take an Uber/taxi* argument again because I've learned with you Knights that I won't win."

"True," he said, knowing he wouldn't have put her into either ride when he could take her to the airport with his driver.

"So I guess this is goodbye." She shifted from foot to foot.

"I was going to go along with you to the airport. Make sure you got off safely." He couldn't help the protectiveness he felt toward her any more than he could deny the desire for her was still there, just as strong as before he'd had her in bed.

"Umm." She pulled her bottom lip with her teeth. "I think we should say goodbye here. You're already home and there's no reason for you to go all the way to the airport." She glanced at him with those big brown eyes that were a window to her soul.

Saying goodbye to him wouldn't be easy.

Having had sex for the first time hadn't been as simple for her as she'd led him to believe.

She wasn't a woman who picked up men on a whim and slept with them, then easily said goodbye the next day.

All things he should have considered, whether or not he'd known she was a virgin. He knew better, but he'd had to have her, and when she'd asked him in, his brain had stopped working. Desire and want had kicked in instead.

But she was right. Saying goodbye here was smarter. Faster. It wouldn't prolong things or send the wrong signal even though his stomach was twisting in knots at the thought.

One night and we tell no one. His stipulation for good reasons. He wasn't going to change the rules now.

"Here. Give me your bag," he said, taking the handle out of her hand. "I'll walk you downstairs." It was the least he could do.

And it would give him another few precious minutes in her presence.

She treated him to a tremulous smile and followed him to the door, then into the hall and to the elevator.

"I hope you enjoyed New York. I am sorry you're leaning toward not coming to school here," he said as the doors opened and they entered the enclosed space.

She tipped her head to one side as if judging the sincerity of his statement. "If I can find something hands-on at home, I think I'll be better off. I just wish I knew what kind of job would be best for me." She shrugged. "I'll figure it out."

"You never wanted to do hotel management?" he asked, knowing her father, Robert Dare, was a hotel magnate.

She shook her head. "That part of the family business isn't for me."

The elevator came to a stop and they stepped into the lobby. He strode past the doorman and led her outside. It was late in the day, almost early evening. The sun had begun dipping behind the buildings, putting a lighter chill in the air.

Ethan caught sight of Mason waiting at the curb, and he paused, not wanting an audience when he said goodbye.

He turned to Sienna to find her waiting, her face turned up to his. "Take care, Sienna. Have a good life."

Dramatic but true. He wouldn't be seeing her again.

Her smile was forced, but he gave her credit, she didn't hesitate. "Bye, Ethan. Be happy."

He wondered if she knew how difficult that emotion was for him to accomplish. Yet in the short time he'd spent with her, he'd been happy. Go figure. A twenty-three-year-old woman had come close to changing his perspective on life after over a year of banging his head against the same brick wall of misery.

She looked up at him expectantly, but he knew better than to kiss her, implying an intimacy that meant something more than what he'd promised or intended.

He leaned forward and kissed her forehead, then walked her to the car, unexpected feelings of regret and disappointment tugging at him as he watched the limo take her away.

Chapter Four

NOT FAR FROM the old Thunder Football Stadium sat the new Thunder Stadium, a glorious, state-of-the-art ode to a team Miami loved. Sienna drove into the old place, where the offices still were, checked in with security, and made her way to Ian's office. She hadn't been summoned, not exactly, but he had called and informed her he'd cleared his morning schedule for an hour so he could hear all about her weekend in Manhattan.

Not *all* about her weekend, she thought, unable to hold back the blush that arose at inopportune moments any time she even thought about Ethan and the hours they'd shared. Her body certainly remembered. She was sore in places she normally never thought about, and she couldn't say she had an ounce of remorse. Except maybe for that lame goodbye.

She wished she'd grabbed him and kissed him the way she'd wanted to instead of letting him get away with a light peck on the forehead like she was someone dear to him. Not someone he'd not only been intimate with but rocked the bedframe with. She might not have much – read any – experience with actual sex, but even she knew what they shared had been spectacular.

She parked her car, pulled on the best neutral face she could muster, and headed to Ian's office. His secretary told her to go on in, so she knocked once and opened the door, not realizing he was on the phone.

He gestured for her to come in and take a seat.

"Well, I'm glad the weekend worked out for you, too. Yes, I agree. She's intelligent and intuitive," Ian said to the person on the phone, giving Sienna a wink as he spoke.

Her stomach flipped over as she realized he must be speaking to Ethan. "Yes. Yes, I agree. Hands-on is always a good thing. I'll consider it," he said, his gaze never leaving hers. "Thanks again for looking out for her."

Sienna did her best not to wince. Ian might just blow a gasket if he knew how much looking … and touching Ethan had actually done.

"Yes. I'll be in touch about the specs and schematics. I have to go. I have an appointment. Goodbye." Ian hung up the phone and met Sienna's gaze. "Well, you made quite an impression."

Forcing a smile, she somehow maintained both her

dignity and composure. "I did my best to represent you. Although… I didn't think you'd be checking up on me with Ethan Knight." She raised her eyebrows at her brother, who liked to have a hand in all his siblings' lives, full and otherwise.

Ian sat on the edge of his desk. "Actually, Ethan called me. He wanted to make sure you had a good weekend that was productive and helpful in making a decision about your future."

Hmm. That was interesting. So it wasn't out of sight, out of mind as she'd assumed. At least she'd had some kind of impact on her *host*.

She cleared her throat. "While touring Manhattan, we talked a lot about what the program offered, and it's honestly just as I thought."

"Meaning?" Ian asked.

"It's more school. Paperwork. Studying. I feel like I'm ready to be out in the world doing things. Making an impact."

He chuckled, probably at her enthusiasm. "Understood. Listen, I have to go over to the construction site … otherwise known as the new stadium to be. Want to join me?" he offered.

"Oh my God, yes!" She jumped up from her seat, eager for the opportunity to check out the new place firsthand, doing her best not to flinch at the shock of slight pain between her legs. No, she wouldn't be forgetting Ethan any time soon.

A little while later, she was wearing a hard hat and walking alongside Ian, touring the first level of the stadium. He pointed out where the concession stands would be, the VIP ticket sales office, and the restrooms. But those things were in any stadium and they weren't Ian's pride and joy.

As he began to speak and point out what was to come, she saw the light in his eyes, unparalleled except when he spoke to or of his pregnant wife, Riley, and his children, Rainey, now four, and Jack, the baby.

He walked her out to the field and began gesturing as he spoke. "Spectators will stand twenty-four feet closer to the field than at the old stadium," he began. "There will be four high-definition video boards on the corners of the upper decks to enhance fan experience, and get this. Two thousand flat-screen monitors spanning the stadium so fans don't miss the action."

"What about suites?" she asked, knowing that was how her father had taken them to football games. No nosebleed seats for the Dares.

"Two hundred and forty modernized, state-of-the-art suites. And for the fans in the stands? Canopy shading for ninety-two percent of the people who come to see the games," he said proudly.

Sienna grinned. "Speaking of fans and fan experience, have you considered a fan suite? You could auction off the ability to have everyday people come, along with, of course, those who can pay. And for those who can't afford it, you can have an online app that accesses the room. Computer terminals for fantasy football."

Ian paused, turning to look at her, caught up in what she was saying.

Emboldened, she went on. "You can hire a company that designs apps to provide a virtual fan experience, installing cameras and digital technology that enable someone to be a player for the day."

He blinked. "Holy shit, Sienna. You're brilliant."

She blushed at the compliment. "I'm just tapping into my age group and what I think people would want while thinking of the marketing standpoint for you."

He grasped her arm and led her away from where there was noisy construction. "I remember when you and Avery put together parties for kids in the cancer ward of the hospital. You made sure the teenagers who couldn't leave had a prom. You were always aware of what people in any situation needed."

"In that case, I just understood better than most. I still volunteer there," she said. "I provide entertainment, books, or whatever they need or might want. I find a way to obtain it for them." Because she knew what it was like to spend ungodly amounts of time in the hospital.

She might have been young but she never forgot. She always remembered there were kids without parents like hers who could afford to be there day and night. Parents who had to work and leave their sick kids alone.

"Of course you do," he said softly. "And you'd better make sure you come to me this year for players to swing by and meet the kids, sign autographs, bring them memorabilia."

She pulled him into an impromptu hug, then quickly released him. Ian wasn't one for a big show of affection but she was. And she appreciated the effort he was making in her life and the things that were important to her.

"As far as the stadium and your ideas, they're damned good ones. You were looking for something valuable to do and contribute without going back to school? I've got it," Ian said. "I want you working hand in hand with whoever we hire. Hell, I want you to find the right people to develop this kind of thing."

She blinked in surprise. "But I don't know the companies."

"My head of tech does. He's just older and doesn't have the unique perspective that you do. Do you have any idea the freshness you can bring to the Thunder?"

"Ummm, no?" But thanks to his excitement, she was beginning to. "But Ian? I heard you on the phone with Ethan. I know he said something to you about me wanting to be hands-on. I don't want a pity job."

She was still surprised Ethan had looked out for her at all.

Ian burst out laughing, a rare feat for the quiet, surly man. "Do I look or act like someone who'd give anyone a pity job? Including family? Just ask Alex how hard he had to work to prove himself to me when he first signed on and you'll have your answer."

She grinned, recalling those early days of her brother, Alex, and the program he'd undertaken with the Thunder to bring concussion awareness to the league along with educating players on post-game life.

"Point taken," she said.

"Okay then. Today you meet with tech. Tomorrow we're meeting with the contractors responsible for wiring. We're going to let them know we may need additional capabilities. "You ready for this?" he asked.

She was soaring with excitement as she answered, "Born ready."

ETHAN DISLIKED BEING summoned, but that's exactly what Ian Dare had done. He wanted a meeting at the stadium to discuss security, and he demanded it on his time frame on his turf. Almost two weeks had passed since Ethan had been with Sienna, and he couldn't get her out of his mind. Traveling to Miami, knowing she was near but he couldn't see her, was driving him to distraction.

Hell, just the memories of her were making him mad. The soft sounds she made when he kissed her, the way her body writhed beneath his when he had her nipple in his mouth, and the tight way she clamped around his dick when he was buried inside her. Then there was her general happiness at everything around her, her overall enjoyment of life, and the laughter she gave so easily. Fuck. His cock was hard at the memory of her.

"Ethan! Jesus, are you listening?" Sebastian, who sat beside him on their private plane, barked at him, snapping his attention back to where it belonged. "Where the fuck have you been for the last couple of weeks? I thought you were a pain before, but lately? I don't even recognize you."

Ethan ran his hand through his hair and glanced at his youngest sibling, who'd put up with a lot from him in the last year. "Sorry, man. Really. I just have a lot on my mind."

Sebastian narrowed his gaze. "I guess I'll have to take that."

It was as much as he could give his brother considering Ethan couldn't possibly tell his sibling that he'd fucked their biggest client's little sister and couldn't get her out of his head.

"Are we ready to deal with Ian?" Sebastian asked.

"Yes." Ethan inclined his head. Business always came first in his mind, and everything he needed, specs included, was front and center. And if he forgot, he had his iPad filled with information.

At Sebastian's second concerned look, Ethan narrowed his gaze. "Have you ever not been able to trust me where business is concerned?"

Sebastian shook his head.

"How's Ashley?" Ethan asked, changing the subject. He glanced out the jet window and realized they were descending.

"Good. I think…" Sebastian paused, his expression carrying a heavy weight.

"Talk to me." Ethan might have had his head up his ass, but he was always there for his brother. "What's wrong?" he pushed when Sebastian didn't answer immediately.

Sebastian gripped the armrest between them. "Ashley wants kids."

"Better you than me," Ethan said, then glanced at his brother and realized how serious this was.

Ethan blew out a long breath, knowing firsthand what kids or at least teenagers demanded. He'd stepped up when his father fell apart and helped with his siblings. Babies, children, were the last thing on his agenda.

But this was Sebastian they were discussing and he was married with a wife he adored, who obviously wanted kids. "And you don't?"

This was a subject never discussed amongst the brothers, although Parker and his wife, Emily, were expecting a baby, as were Sierra and her husband.

"What if I fuck it up?" Sebastian asked. "After all, look at the example I had. Pay for it and it'll get better," he muttered resentfully.

Sebastian was an interesting case. When he was a kid, their father had bought him out of a lot of problems, choosing to throw money at any given situation instead of being a parent. As a result, Sebastian had thought he could charm his way through life. He'd recently learned otherwise and reunited with Ashley, who'd lived with them for a brief time during one of his father's even briefer marriages. After screwing up big-time when they were kids, Ashley had returned after Mandy died and Sebastian had had to make it up to Ashley before she'd even give him the time of day. He'd manned up and they'd been happily married ever since.

But Ethan could understand his brother's fears. "Just do the opposite of what Dad would do," Ethan said. "That's how I stepped up and helped raise all of you."

A wry smile twisted Sebastian's lips. "You did, didn't you? Not even two years older than Parker and you were everything to us."

Ethan's chest warmed at the appreciation in his brother's tone. He hadn't done it for the accolades. His siblings had needed him but it was nice to be appreciated.

"You'll be a great father. I know it. You just need to believe in yourself. I believe in you and I know Ashley does, too."

Sebastian let out a huge breath of air. "Wow. I didn't realize I was holding that in."

Ethan frowned. "Maybe I was too caught up in my own shit over the last year to realize you needed me."

Sebastian rolled his eyes. "You're entitled to take time for yourself. Let's face it. Mandy fucked you over. If you needed to pull back to get past it, nobody blames you."

Ethan nodded. But he was slowly coming back to himself, he thought, and he had a little sprite of a woman who'd spent all of twenty-four hours with him to thank.

And he was back to thinking of Sienna. This time it was Ethan gripping the armrest of his seat, because no matter what had occurred between them, it was over. Ethan was by no means ready for any kind of relationship and Sienna had commitment kind of girl

69

written all over her pretty face.

✦   ✦   ✦

SIENNA HAD ACCOMPLISHED a lot in her two weeks working under Ian, although he'd handed over preliminary approval on things to his sister Olivia, the executive director of the Miami Thunder. Sienna wasn't as close with Olivia as she was with Avery, but they had a good personal relationship and were gaining an even better one by working together. She'd pulled the other woman into the minute details of her ideas, and together they'd formed a partnership of sorts that worked. Considering this was a last-minute add-on to the stadium as a whole, they'd made a good start, including hiring an internet company that could oversee and help implement the apps and make Sienna's ideas reality.

She walked into the old stadium and headed directly for Olivia's office, bypassing the brunch that had been set up for guests. The smell of the bacon had her stomach churning and it wasn't a pleasant sensation. She hadn't felt well the last couple of days, either, and she figured she'd picked up a virus or something.

She walked into the office to find Olivia eating an egg sandwich, and that triggered her gag reflex. "Excuse me."

She ran for the nearest ladies' room, making it just

in time. Pulling herself together, she washed up and dug a breath mint out of her purse before heading back to Olivia's office.

"Are you okay?" Olivia perched her glasses on her head and met Sienna's gaze with a concerned look on her face.

Sienna nodded. "I think I have a bug or something. I may just go home early."

Olivia's gaze softened. "You should do that. I think Ian just wants us to stop by and meet the people he's invited for a big stadium meeting. I'm sure you can slip out right after."

"I can do that." The imminent nausea had passed. "Do you know who he's hosting?" Sienna placed her handbag onto a chair and settled into the seat beside it.

"The company in charge of security and smart tech at the new stadium." Olivia glanced at the computer screen by her desk. "Ethan and Sebastian Knight."

If Sienna hadn't just thrown up, she might have lost it anyway, hearing that Ethan was in the building and Ian expected them to meet. Of course, her half brother had no idea that there was any more between Sienna and Ethan than a casual acquaintance from their brief weekend together.

"You look like you're going to be sick again," Olivia said, brows furrowing.

"No. I'm okay." She was now forewarned, which

she appreciated. She'd have a few precious minutes to come to terms with seeing him again and pretend he'd been nothing more to her than a good host.

Not the man she'd propositioned. Who she'd lost her virginity to. Sat half-naked with while they devoured Chinese food. Slept wrapped in his arms. And had woken up to find him thrusting inside her, then climaxing all over her back.

God.

Were the recollections still as vivid for him as they were for her? Did he wake up thinking about their time together and fall asleep the same way? Did he wrap his hand around his thick cock and make himself come to the memories of their bodies grinding together? Because she did variations of all those things.

And yet she had to face him again now and pretend he was a business associate of Ian's she barely knew. To her surprise, the thought of him looking right through her hurt more than it should given their agreement.

One time and nobody would ever know.

"Ready?" Olivia asked, placing her glasses onto her face and rising from her seat.

"Of course." Sienna picked up her handbag and followed Olivia out of the office, doing her best to pull herself together and lock away any sexy thoughts of Ethan Knight.

✧　✧　✧

ETHAN DIDN'T NEED to be wined and dined, or in this case fed breakfast, while meeting some of the major league football stars who played for the Miami Thunder. Although he realized this wasn't geared toward him but was a corresponding photo opp and charity breakfast, and it was probably easier for Ian to meet them here before heading over to the new stadium for a walk-through and meeting.

Ian strode over and greeted Ethan and Sebastian, shaking their hands and slapping them on the backs as if they were old friends working on a joint project. Which, Ethan supposed, they were. It wouldn't pay for him to be his grumpy, pissy self with the man he needed to please with both his security and smart technology.

Ian began to discuss a new addition to the fan experience, something his team would need to get up to speed with. Sebastian talked, and Ethan listened, content to let his brother run the show. Sebastian had always been the schmoozer, the brother with the personality and ability to charm everyone they worked with and reassure people when something went wrong. It made sense to let him convince Ian that Knight Time Technology could handle this admittedly comprehensive idea for including a virtual fan experience at the stadium. KTT could work alongside the computer company that created the apps and make sure the wireless technology was secure.

"Aah, here she is," Ian said, gesturing toward the entrance to the large conference room. "The woman responsible for the entire fan-experience idea. Ethan, you know my half sister, Sienna."

Ethan heard her name, the sound both a shock to his system and a punch in the gut at the same time. He hadn't expected to see Sienna again ever, especially not during his time in Miami. But here she was, walking over with a smile on her face.

"And Sienna, this is Ethan's brother, Sebastian. And Sebastian, Ethan, this is my other sister, our executive director, Olivia Rhodes." Ian gestured to the woman standing beside Sienna, a brunette who bore a striking resemblance to her brother.

But the introductions went over Ethan's head because his gaze was wholly focused on the woman he couldn't get out of his mind. Sienna appeared as beautiful as he remembered but much more fragile. Her skin was pale, her eyes wide as she forced a smile and shook Sebastian's hand first.

"Nice to meet you," she said.

"Same." Sebastian, unaware of Ethan's reeling emotions, turned to Olivia Rhodes, giving her the same greeting.

"Ethan, you mentioned to me that Sienna was interested in more hands-on business dealings than school," Ian said. "And when she returned from her weekend in New York, she blew me away with her ideas. Once we hired a company to implement the concepts, I thought it prudent to bring you in for security."

"I'm impressed with her plans, as well," Ethan said, not surprised at her ingenuity and intelligence. It had just been a question of finding the right fit for her business-wise. Apparently Ian had seen and tapped into the potential.

"So Sienna told me all about your weekend together in Manhattan."

"We … kept busy," Ethan muttered.

Sienna flushed a deep shade of red, and he quickly looked away, not wanting to draw attention to them.

"Right, we did." Sienna gestured with her hands in that expressive way he'd found so engaging in New York. "The gala was lovely but I especially enjoyed seeing the sights. The Statue of Liberty was fascinating and One World Trade was heart-wrenching. In addition, we had good talks and it was very productive for me."

Listening to her sum up their weekend into one of sightseeing and productivity had Ethan clenching his teeth in frustration considering he knew he'd spent much of that time balls deep inside her.

"We had a nice time, didn't we … Ethan?" She hesitated, stumbling over his name.

If she'd called him Mr. Knight, he didn't know if he'd have been able to restrain himself from throwing her over his shoulder and storming out of here like a caveman so he could take her in the nearest office he could find.

"It was fucking wonderful," he muttered.

Sebastian turned to him, mouth open, and Ethan realized his mistake immediately.

"I mean it was great. We had fun," Ethan said, rushing to be more polite and diplomatic. "And I'm sure there won't be any issues on the project going forward." Stick to business, he reminded himself.

"No, there won't be," Ian said.

"And we're aware that we need a project manager on site. Especially now that we're in the building phase," Sebastian said, citing what, to Ethan, was a sticky subject.

The last big contract they'd had, Ethan had sent a willing Mandy to handle the job in LA and she'd betrayed them all, buying substandard products and indulging in her drug addiction and affair. Finding someone to stay in Miami? Ethan had put off thinking about it at all.

Sebastian stepped forward. "I was going to offer to

come down during the week and fly back to New York on the weekends." He ran a hand over the back of his neck, his reluctance to take on this job real. He had Ashley at home… and apparently they had big discussions going on about having a family. But as a team player, Sebastian's offer was genuine.

"Still a newlywed," Ethan said, grinning at his sibling, not wanting Ian Dare to worry about anything when it came to KTT's handling of this deal. "I wouldn't ask you to do that," he reassured Sebastian.

But he wasn't going to send just anyone to oversee such an important project. He'd already found out what happened when he wasn't hands-on.

"So what do you suggest?" Sebastian asked. "Parker has moved to Colorado to run his new ski shops. Who else can we trust?"

"I'll do it. I'll stay in Miami for the duration of our role in the construction," Ethan said.

Beside him, Sienna sucked in a startled gasp.

Unaware of the undercurrents or implications of Ethan's decision for Sienna, Ian nodded, relief in his gaze.

"But" – Sebastian glanced at Ethan – "the office…"

"It's not like I can't run the business from here, and you're in New York for anything that comes up there. It's decided," he said, folding his arms across his chest.

Without looking directly at Sienna, he was still aware of her shock at his declaration. He felt the same damned way. He couldn't be around her without wanting her. He didn't know how he'd be in Miami and stay away.

"As long as that's decided, let's go take a look at the new stadium," Ian said. "Are you ladies coming?" he asked Olivia and Sienna.

"I'll join you," Olivia said. "I haven't been over in a while."

"Sienna?" Ian asked.

She drew a deep breath. "Actually I wasn't feeling well this morning. I think I'm going to take the rest of the day off, if you don't mind."

"Of course I don't mind. Go on home and feel better," Ian said.

She said her goodbyes and walked out.

Ethan was unable to tear his gaze from her ass as she left the room, his gaze narrowed at her abrupt departure. If she hadn't been pale when she walked in, Ethan would think she was avoiding him.

"Before we go over to the stadium, can we have a word?" Sebastian asked him.

"I need to talk to a few people, so take your time." Ian strode off, Olivia walking alongside him.

Sebastian grabbed his arm and pulled him to the side, where they could talk alone. "What's going on with you?"

"What do you mean?" Ethan thought he'd kept it together pretty damned well considering all he'd wanted was to be alone with Sienna.

"It was *fucking wonderful?* That's how you refer to spending the weekend with our biggest client's sister?" Sebastian sounded horrified.

"It was better than saying we spent the weekend fucking," he muttered and his brother's gaze went wide.

"Jesus Christ, you didn't?" Sebastian looked Ethan in the eye. "You did. Son of a bitch. What were you thinking?"

"Clearly I wasn't." Not with the right head, anyway.

"So that's what's been on your mind. Why you can't concentrate on business." Sebastian glanced across the room.

Ethan did the same and caught sight of Ian talking to one of the players.

"And you're sure you want to stay here and oversee this project? Or is she the reason you're willing to do it?" Sebastian asked, his tone low.

"One of us needs to be here and it makes sense that it's me. Can we let the rest go for now?" He wasn't ready to think about why he was so willing to find himself in Miami for the next couple of months.

Not when he already knew the answer.

Chapter Five

S IENNA SPENT THE weekend doing ordinary things in a state of disbelief. She cleaned her apartment, folded her laundry, went grocery shopping … all the while knowing that Ethan was back in New York, getting himself settled so he could be in Miami tonight or tomorrow morning. And somehow, Ian had gotten it into his head that Sienna and her fan-experience app and ideas meant she had to work with him while he was in town overseeing his part in the stadium project.

Ian had no idea what he was asking of her. It had been hard enough being in the same room with Ethan, pretending they were mere acquaintances, when she'd felt him inside her body. When she wanted him to take her again. Feelings that she didn't get the notion, during the brief time she'd been with Ethan in the conference room, were reciprocated. He'd been cool and aloof. Very much the man in charge, and he'd sounded like his time with her had been nothing but a chore.

She ran a hand along her damp neck. The temperature had soared to one hundred and two degrees outside, and the sun was baking through the window, so the air conditioning pumping away in her small apartment unit wasn't cooling her off as much as she would have liked. At this point she was wearing a pair of boy shorts and matching sports bra without a top because it was that hot. She pulled her hair into a high, messy bun and settled on the couch. Tonight was a pizza night, no cooking or turning on the oven and making this place even warmer.

She retrieved an app and ordered herself an individual pie, plain because the weirdest things were making her nauseous, along with two cans of Coke, and settled in to wait for the delivery. While she sat, she made notes on ideas she had to enhance the fan experience at the stadium, both in person and in the virtual realm.

When her doorbell rang, she jumped up, surprised her dinner had arrived so soon but more than happy because she was starving. Without checking the peephole, she flung the door open … and came face-to-face with Ethan.

He didn't look like the Ethan Knight she'd grown used to. He wasn't wearing a suit, nor was he in a pair of dress pants and shirt. Instead, he wore khaki cargo shorts and a tee shirt, and she had to admit she liked the look on him. Add the scruff on his face and the gleaming look in his eyes and he was one sexy-ass man.

"You're not the pizza deliveryman."

He braced a hand on the doorframe. "Disappointed?" he asked.

She swallowed hard. "No. Just shocked."

She gestured for him to enter, but his gaze swept over her, taking in her barely there outfit.

He let out one of those low growls she'd come to recognize as acknowledgment of his arousal and she blinked in surprise. She really had thought he was no longer interested.

"Get inside," he muttered. "Before someone sees you."

"It's warm out," she said, justifying her clothing when it was none of his business what she wore.

"The delivery boy doesn't need to see your tight, hot little body." He backed her into the apartment and shut the door behind them. "It's for my eyes alone."

The predatory sound in his voice matched the proprietary look in his eyes, and her arousal immediately spiked. Desire ratcheted up inside her, want dampening her underwear. Jesus. The man was potent. And she couldn't deny how much she desired him.

He reached for her, his big hand wrapping around her neck as he pulled her close and sealed his lips over hers. She moaned and slid her tongue over his mouth, demanding entrance, taking *her* due. This time it wasn't all about him calling the shots. She'd been with him before, and he appreciated when she was bold and asked for what she wanted. Like when she'd invited him to stay. His eyes had glittered a deeper blue.

"Fuck, I missed you." The words spilled out of him, and if they sounded reluctant, she pushed the thought away, only caring about the here and now.

He kissed her, his mouth devouring hers, sucking on her tongue, the passion flowing back and forth between them. Somehow they ended up on the couch, him pushing her down, his body crushing hers into the cushions. His hard cock pressed insistently against her core, and a rush of wetness coated her underwear once more. His hips ground into hers while he pushed her hair off her face with his hands and continued to brand her with his mouth.

She arched her hips and rubbed her sex against his erection, the pulsing feeling of a climax rushing at her quickly and unexpectedly. She threaded her fingers through his hair and held on as he ground his cock into her and she flew apart beneath him. Wave after wave of trembling sensation racked her body as she came.

He rocked himself into her until the shaking subsided, and with a groan, he rose to his feet. He yanked his wallet out of his pocket, pulled a condom from inside it, and undressed in the blink of an eye. She did the same, shimmying the tight shorts down and off her legs, pulling her panties off with them.

He slid on protection, then sat down on the couch and shifted her to her knees, facing him, her thighs on either side of his. He gripped his cock, pumping his hand up and down the straining shaft, then helped her position herself over him.

Next thing she knew, he was filling her, thick, hard, and deep, as she lowered herself completely. She braced her hands on his shoulders and stilled, her gaze meeting his. It was intimate, her entire body aware of him inside her.

"Move," he said, his voice husky and raw.

She lifted herself up, felt the drag of his erection as he pulled out of her. His hands held on to her hips and he began to direct her movements, gliding her up and down his shaft. Instinct had her lifting and dropping her body in time to the shifting of his hips, pure need had her rocking her clit against him with every joining of their bodies, and suddenly the impossible began to happen.

A small stirring of another climax started deep inside her, one that grew with every thrust and grind, and suddenly she was there, coming again, harder, more deeply, feeling every inch of him as he groaned and followed her up and over into utter ecstasy.

She collapsed against him, her muscles suddenly no longer able to hold her up, and she buried her face in his neck, inhaling his musky, masculine scent and getting lost in the smell and feel of him around her.

The sudden sound of the doorbell intruded, and he uttered a curse, pushing her off him. "Coming!" he yelled out, buying them time. "Go." He gestured and she grabbed her clothing and ran for the bathroom, leaving him to ditch the condom, get dressed, and rescue her dinner.

Body sore, cheeks flaming, she rejoined him in the family room, where he'd put the pizza on the table by the sofa.

"Umm, want dinner?" she asked, unsure what the protocol was in a situation like this.

He nodded, so she headed to the kitchen, returning with plates, napkins, and cups.

Next thing she knew, she was sitting cross-legged on the sofa, devouring first one, then two, then a third slice of pizza, hunger returning where it hadn't existed for the last couple of days.

He ate his own slices.

She didn't count how many, but she couldn't miss the amused grin on his handsome face.

"I have no clue where you're putting all that food," he muttered.

She blushed in embarrassment. "A gentleman

wouldn't mention it, you know."

He rolled his shoulders dismissively. "Did I ever claim to be a gentleman?" To her surprise, he winked at her and took a long sip of his soda.

Finished now, she slid her plate away and glanced over at him. "Is Sebastian your only brother?" She decided she was going to ask about his family. His life. How else could she get to know this enigmatic man?

He wiped his face with a napkin and placed his plate on top of hers. "Youngest. There's my middle brother, Parker, who went to Colorado recently to scope out a resort for a corporate retreat, met a woman, and never left, and Sierra, who you've met."

She nodded.

"How about you?" he asked. "I know Ian and I met Olivia. Who else is there?"

She couldn't help it. She burst out laughing. "Let's see. If you haven't heard the story of the infamous Robert Dare, this is how it goes. My father married his first wife as part of a business deal. They had Ian, Tyler, Scott, Olivia, and Avery. Early on during their marriage, he met my mom and they had an affair." She winced at the revelation that never felt good. "That resulted in a second family. Alex, Jason, and me." She waved her hand in the air. "The baby of the group."

"Holy shit." Ethan ran a hand through his long hair and shook his head. "Soap opera land."

"You can say that again. Anyway, that's how many siblings I have, half and full. The rest of the story is for another day and time." Nobody got the full lowdown on her childhood illness unless they were in her life to stay.

Rising from her seat, she picked up their plates and cleaned up the table. Ethan helped, taking the pizza box and the soda cans and carrying them into the kitchen.

She had no idea where things stood between them, but after tonight, a feeling of hope bloomed inside her chest. Not only had he come after her, they couldn't keep their hands off each other. Surely that meant something.

She bit down on her lower lip and he noticed, pulling at it until she released her teeth. "Stop that. You're giving me ideas," he said gruffly. Leaning down, he slicked his tongue over her abused lip. "I can't keep my hands off you." The slide of his tongue turned into a prolonged kiss, one that had her grasping at his shirt and hanging on for the ride.

By the time he released her, she was panting and ready to go again, although the soreness between her thighs was begging her to reconsider.

"So I've been thinking," he said.

"Yes?" She leaned against the granite countertop in her kitchen.

"Since I'm going to be here for a while and this thing between us isn't going away, what do you say we hook up while I'm here?"

She tipped her head to one side. "Hook up," she reiterated, to make sure they were on the same page. In her mind, that meant just sex. No relationship, no dating. No commitment.

She stared at him until he got the message and began to elaborate.

"Right. While I'm in town, we'll get together. Like this." He gestured between them, indicating what had happened on the sofa earlier.

"So … just sex," she said, needing to be clear.

"Exactly."

Her stomach plummeted at his affirmation. She hadn't planned on riding off into the sunset with the man, but she had hoped for … more. A dinner. A date. Something beyond a meaningless hookup.

Before she could fully wrap her mind around what he was proposing, something that hurt but that she might be able to work with – after all, what started out as casual could definitely turn into something more – he spoke again.

"And no one can know about us. I'm all about keeping business and pleasure separate, and in this case, I can't afford to fuck up this deal because your brother loses his mind if he finds out about us."

Pain lanced through her. If there was one thing he could have said to kill anything between them, that was it. "So you're proposing a secret relationship."

"Yes."

"Like the kind my mother had with my father."

He narrowed his gaze, obviously now realizing he had opened a can of worms he hadn't intended. "Not really. For one thing, I'm not married."

She perched her hands on her hips. "Then why keep us a secret if we're two consenting adults?" She raised her eyebrows, pinning him in place. "Unless you're ashamed of being with me?"

"No but–"

"Get out." Her heart beat painfully and furiously inside her chest. She honestly didn't give a rat's ass why he was proposing a dirty little secret relationship. Just the fact that he didn't think enough of her to offer more was reason enough to throw him the hell out now.

He stepped closer, remorse in his gaze. "Sienna, look, you have to see things from my perspective."

"The hell I do." She narrowed her gaze, her hand reaching for the nearest item on the counter and coming up with a salt shaker. "I'm asking you one last time to go."

"And I want you to see how good we could be during the time we have."

That was it. Her fingers curled around the ceramic piece and she threw it at him, hitting him in the shoulder, before it bounced off and landed uselessly on the floor.

He looked at her, shock in his expression. "I—"

"Get the hell out, Ethan."

Very slowly, his gaze never leaving hers, he bent down and picked up the salt shaker, placing it on the table behind him. Then he backed away, walking out while shaking his head like only a blind, foolish man could do.

✧   ✧   ✧

THAT HAD BEEN a fuckup to end all fuckups, Ethan thought. His hand went to where the hard salt shaker had hit him on the shoulder, and despite it all, he grinned at Sienna's spirit and spunk. She hadn't taken his shit and he had to admire that about her. But he'd wanted to make her understand his reasoning.

So you should have started out explaining, not asking for a hookup like a dumb-ass teenage boy. He clenched his jaw at his own idiocy. Being around her made him stupid. All reason and common sense went out the window. The man who could negotiate billion-dollar business deals couldn't even make one tiny woman see reason.

Still, now that he gave it thought, he understood how bad his proposal looked from her point of view.

She had just told him about her family situation. He should have phrased things much differently, because from his perspective, a secret affair made pure business sense. Ian Dare wasn't going to stand by and let him date – in her own words – the baby of the family.

Not that dating was on his agenda, and that was the point. He was dark; she was light. Sienna didn't need to be dragged into his murky life, not when he couldn't see past the pain of his marriage and the betrayal he hadn't seen coming.

She might not be interested in his proposition, but he sure as hell couldn't stay away from her or she from him. Which should make working together extremely interesting.

SIENNA WOKE UP the morning after Ethan left feeling nauseous again and a little dizzy. She was definitely going to have to make a doctor's appointment and find out why she couldn't seem to come to herself. In the meantime, she had a meeting scheduled with Olivia and the app developers at the stadium that she couldn't miss.

Skipping breakfast because she wasn't sure she could keep it down, she stood in front of her closet and chose a sundress in deference to the sticky, hot weather that persisted, along with a pair of low heels, and headed to work.

As her luck was running, she pulled into a parking spot at the same time as Ethan, who'd obviously rented a car for his time here. She climbed out of her Jeep and met up with him as they walked toward the entrance.

"Good morning," he said, his gaze raking over her, his expression filled with male appreciation. "You're looking good."

She narrowed her gaze through her sunglasses. She couldn't believe he was going to act like nothing had happened last night.

Yes, yes she could.

"Not speaking to me?" he asked, picking up his pace to keep up with her.

And deliberately, she'd bet, brushing his arm against hers as they walked. "Of course not. That would be childish." She wished she could hold a grudge.

She wanted to maintain both her anger and her distance. What he'd offered her last night had been insulting and hurtful, more so because he'd just been deep inside her body and, she admitted, because she'd let herself believe that him showing up at her apartment meant more than it had.

She wouldn't make that mistake again.

He opened the door and let her step inside, and

she welcomed the cool rush of air that greeted her. They walked past the huge blown-up photographs of the stars of the Miami Thunder and toward the office area.

"I'm going to check in with Ian. He said he'd get me set up in an office for the duration," Ethan said.

They stopped by the outer area of Ian's office. His secretary sat right inside.

She forced a smile. "I'm sure he'll make certain you're well taken care of."

"Where's your office?" Ethan asked.

She wished she could tell him that information was on a need-to-know basis... and he didn't need to know. But again, that would be acting infantile, and she had no choice but to treat him like an adult and an important member of the team she'd been hired to work on.

"I'm over there." She gestured down the hall. "Olivia and I share a tandem office. She had extra room and that's where they put me."

Feeling light-headed, she leaned against the wall, letting the coolness from the wall seep into her skin.

"What's wrong?" he immediately asked, his hand coming to her waist.

She wished she could shrug it off, but that would be too much motion right now. "I'm just a little dizzy. I'll be fine." Except she wasn't.

The only warning she got was a buzzing in her ears and a rush of sensation to her head before she realized she was about to faint.

"I need to sit." Before he could react, she lowered herself to the ground, hoping to prevent the inevitable, but the next thing she knew, she blacked out.

ETHAN GRABBED SIENNA'S body before she hit the floor, her muscles giving out on her as she collapsed into his arms. He managed to ease her down without her head taking a hit on the wall or the ground.

"Ian!" Panicked but keeping his wits about him, he called for her brother, who Ethan knew was already in his office behind them.

He heard noise from the other side of the wall and then Ian appeared, taking in the situation immediately.

"Dorothy, call 911," he yelled into the office, then knelt down beside them. "What happened?"

"She leaned against the wall, said she was dizzy, and next thing I knew, she was out." Ethan stroked her hair off her face and noticed her lashes fluttering as she came back to herself.

"Oh my God. Did I faint?" Sienna struggled to sit, but Ethan kept a tight hold on her.

"Don't move too quickly. You're likely to pass out again."

Ian grasped her hand. "What happened?"

She shrugged. "I haven't been feeling well. I came in for the meeting anyway and I got dizzy."

"Have you eaten today?" Ethan asked.

She shook her head. "I was nauseous this morning."

Ethan frowned. In the two weeks since he'd seen her in New York, he noticed she looked more fragile, like she'd lost some weight, but then last night she'd devoured three slices of pizza like a person starved. He hadn't given it another thought.

"I called 911," Ian's secretary, a young redheaded woman, stuck her head out the door and said.

"Oh no. That's not necessary. I'm feeling better already."

"Too bad," Ethan said, his tone making it clear he wouldn't accept an argument.

"I agree." Ian patted her hand. "Given everything in your past, better safe than sorry."

Her glare at him could cut ice, and Ethan knew he wouldn't be getting an explanation about what Ian had been referring to. Not that he wouldn't try for one later.

Right now he was worried about Sienna.

"What's going on?" Olivia rushed out of the office at the far end of the hall and joined everyone surrounding Sienna. She and Ian shot each other concerned glances which made Ethan uneasy.

Finally, the paramedics showed up, took her blood pressure, pronounced it low, and at Ian's insistence, they took Sienna to the hospital for tests. Because he whispered with the paramedics, Ethan still didn't know what the main concern was; however, he agreed she needed to be looked at by a doctor.

It was on the tip of his tongue to insist he'd ride with her in the ambulance, except he realized how ridiculous he would look and that doing such a thing would shine a spotlight on his relationship with Sienna. The exact thing he'd been trying to avoid by suggesting a secret affair.

He scowled, watching as Ian climbed into the back with his half sister and accompanied her to the hospital. Although Ethan was worried about how it would look, he headed to his car and drove directly to the emergency room anyway, wanting to know if she was okay. Considering she'd collapsed in his arms, he didn't think anyone would question his presence there.

In the waiting area, he met up with Olivia and Ian. Obviously the family phone chain had been active on the ride over because, one by one, men and women with the familiar Dare features strode into the room and were filled in on what they knew so far.

Which was nothing yet.

He noted that everyone in the room was young,

which meant they were siblings. Over time, others arrived, too, spouses of Sienna's brothers and sisters. This family definitely hovered over one of their own. Then again, if Sierra ended up in a hospital, all of her brothers would be there in a heartbeat.

Finally, there was a slightly older woman with blonde hair, who definitely resembled Sienna, sitting in the corner. Ethan pegged the woman as Sienna's mother. Only Alex Dare, who Ethan recognized from his football-playing days, and a blonde woman Ethan assumed was his wife, comforted her.

Recalling the family dynamic and explanation he'd been given last night, Ethan realized the full-blooded Dares might be close with Sienna, but her mother was still the outsider. The other woman. The dirty little secret.

He muttered a curse aimed at himself, as he realized just why Sienna had reacted the way she had to his proposition.

Now that the excitement of her initial fainting had worn off and the large group of Dares congregated together, Ethan was left alone with his thoughts, and they weren't good ones. Hospitals reminded him of Mandy. There had been her shoulder surgery and the opioids she'd been given as painkillers after.

She'd gotten addicted and Ethan had been too preoccupied with work to notice. Then the long months she'd been in California overseeing the Keystone project. Even when they'd seen each other in between, he hadn't realized she wasn't herself. Or if he had, he'd been too busy to really notice what was in front of him. Until the night he'd come home and tried to wake her up. Except she'd overdosed and was dead. He shuddered at the memory, not liking how Sienna's passing out in his arms had taken him back to that time.

"How are you holding up?" Olivia Rhodes had walked over and asked, obviously taking pity on him.

"I'm fine. Just concerned about Sienna, like everyone else," he said.

Olivia nodded in agreement. "You caught her before she fell. If not for you, she might have hit her head. Then we'd have a concussion to deal with on top of whatever else, so thank you."

"I just happened to be in the right place at the right time." He ducked his head, not meeting her gaze, afraid he'd give something away.

Before she could reply, a doctor in a white medical jacket walked into the room. "Sienna Dare's family?"

The entire room lifted their heads.

"She'd like to see her mother."

"Is she okay?" Ian strode over to the doctor, his domineering presence all but demanding answers.

The older man tipped his head. "And you are?"

"Her brother. Now is she okay?"

The other man nodded. "She is. Preliminary bloodwork is all good. She asked me to tell you all that. Now is her mother here? She said she'd asked someone to call her."

The woman who Ethan had thought was Sienna's mom rose from her seat and headed back to see her daughter.

Ian began pacing, and this time it was Ethan who took pity on someone.

He walked over and faced the other man. "Is there anything I can do?" It seemed like a ridiculous question considering an entire horde of people were here who were closer to Sienna than Ethan.

Ian tipped his head and Ethan followed him to a private corner of the room. "I'm sure you're wondering why the entire family would show up over a simple fainting spell?"

"I didn't think it was my business to ask, but yes. My brothers would be there for my sister but this is…"

"Excessive?"

Ethan chuckled. "You could say that."

"Sienna had childhood leukemia," Ian said, and all the air left Ethan's lungs.

"I'm sorry, what?" He had to have heard wrong.

Ian merely nodded. His hands in his pants pocket,

his stress very raw and real. "Leukemia. Ultimately we were all tested and Avery was a match. She donated bone marrow and saved Sienna's life."

Ethan needed a chair because he thought it likely he might faint. His fragile, beautiful woman had endured all that as a child?

"I had no idea."

"She doesn't like to talk about it with just anyone. She feels like she's put it behind her and only wants to focus on the present and the future."

Head still spinning, Ethan said, "I understand that."

"I appreciate you coming. I know this isn't what you signed on for when you said you'd stay to oversee the stadium project."

Ethan lowered himself into a chair and Ian followed, sitting beside him. "The Knights are very family oriented. I understand," he assured the man. "The doctor said the preliminary bloodwork was good?" Ethan needed to be certain he'd heard correctly.

"Yes." Ian let out a relieved breath. "We have no reason to believe it will come back. It's been fifteen years. But we still tend to panic. And baby her." He ran a hand through his hair. "I ... I was the worst behaved when I found out that my father had other children. Another family. And I didn't come around until just recently. Ever since Riley opened my eyes, I've been trying to more than make up for my behavior."

"Did I hear my name?" A curvy brunette with wavy hair and a bright smile strode up to Ian and put her hand in his.

"Ethan Knight, this is my wife, Riley Dare. I was just explaining our complicated family dynamic to a man who is supposed to be a business associate. But he caught Sienna when she fainted, so he's here and learning more about the Dares than he probably cares to know." Ian shook his head, a wry smile twisting his mouth.

Little did Ian know, Ethan savored every word of explanation he received on Sienna and her background. He catalogued it in his mind. He set it aside to consider and think about later.

All he could do now was breathe a sigh of relief … and wish he could go back and see for himself that she was okay.

Chapter Six

"I'M PREGNANT," SIENNA told her mother, who stood at her bedside, hand in hers. She still couldn't say the words and process them in her mind.

Her mother clasped her hand tighter. "We'll figure it out, baby. Whatever you want to do, I'll support you."

Sienna leaned back against the pillow and groaned in relief. The one thing about Savannah Sheppard Dare was that her kids could talk to her about anything. And when the doctor told Sienna the fainting had been caused by a drop in blood pressure due to her pregnancy, once she'd gotten over the shock, she'd wanted to tell her mother.

From the time she was old enough to understand, she'd been told the chances of her having a child were slim to none. That the chemotherapy and the stem cell transplant had probably ended those chances, and she thought she'd come to terms with that. To be told she was pregnant?

Nothing short of mind-blowing. She'd never let

herself want kids because she'd been told it hadn't been in the cards. But now? She put her hand over her stomach, feeling a fierce protectiveness she hadn't known she was capable of… along with a sense of excitement that had her wanting to share the news with the world.

She had thought about confiding in Avery, her best friend as well as half sister, but that would put Avery in a rough spot because in no way could Sienna let Ian find out. Not yet. Nobody could know until the Knight Time Technology part of the new stadium was complete and Ian couldn't throw Ethan off the project for knocking up his baby sister.

"So … anything more you want to tell me?" her mother asked, her tone wise.

Sienna grinned. "Well, there's a man–"

"I would assume so." Her mom treated her to a warm smile. "Is this man going to step up and do the right thing?"

Sienna shrugged, pure terror racing through her veins at the thought of telling Ethan she was having his baby. She didn't think the man who wanted a secret affair would be thrilled to discover he was going to be a father. But her heart told her he was also a decent guy who she didn't think would abandon his child.

As far as the woman who came along with said

baby? Well, that was another story, considering he wasn't interested in a real relationship with her at all.

"I don't know enough about him to answer that," she hedged for now. "But I don't want to tell him just yet, anyway."

Her mom opened her mouth to argue, and Sienna said, "I will tell him. I won't keep it a secret forever. It's just that he's a part of Ian's stadium project and I don't want to be the cause of yet more Dare drama." Because if Ian found out she'd slept with Ethan Knight and he'd gotten her pregnant, he would lose his ever-loving mind. He'd blame Ethan and throw him and his company out, and she knew this contract was important to both of them. She just needed to buy some time.

Her mother frowned. "Secrets are bad, honey. We all know this firsthand," Savannah said.

"And sometimes the truth is worse. Look what finding out about my leukemia did to the whole family. It destroyed Ian's side."

Savannah winced. "I know how awful it was. I know I shouldn't have let things go on with Robert, but I can't regret my babies. My family."

"I know, Mom." Sienna didn't agree with her mother's actions. She didn't condone cheating any more than she'd have approved of breaking up Ian's side of the family. The situation sucked and her father was as much to blame as anyone. "But the facts are the facts. I know what happened and why. I won't let Ian's project be undermined because of me. I'll tell him when the time is right."

"Tell who what?" Ian asked, pushing his way into the room, a harried, unhappy nurse at his heels.

"Sir, I told you, one visitor at a time."

As if Ian Dare ever thought the rules applied to him. "Let him stay, please?"

Savannah rose to her feet. "I should go." She leaned down and kissed Sienna's cheek. "I'll be in touch, and if you need me, you call me." She glanced at Ian. "Thank you for looking out for my daughter."

Ian nodded stiffly.

It pained Sienna but there was nothing she could do to fix this particular relationship.

"So what's going on?" Ian asked.

Sienna drew a deep breath. "Low blood sugar, apparently. I hadn't eaten and I just got light-headed and passed out." She shrugged. "I'm really sorry I gave everyone such a scare. I know they're probably all out in the waiting room worrying."

His expression softened. "Well, you did let the doctor tell us that your bloodwork looked good, so they're calmer. Most have left and said they'd call you later when you were released and back home."

"Okay."

"There is someone who hasn't left."

She tilted her head to the side. "Who's that?"

"The man who caught you when you fainted. Ethan Knight."

Her eyes opened wide and she let out a surprised breath of air, but she had no idea what to say.

"I think he feels responsible for you." Ian shook his head and laughed. "You know, save a life and all that?"

She rolled her eyes. "I wouldn't go that far. He just kept my head from exploding on the ground. Said like that, I guess it's a pretty big deal."

"I think you gave him a scare," Ian said.

That wasn't the only thing she'd be giving him, she thought, holding back a laugh of hysteria. She still hadn't come to terms with the notion of having a baby herself.

She could only imagine what Ethan's reaction was going to be when he found out.

"Would you mind if he came in? Saw for himself you were okay? I think he'll be more comfortable leaving then," Ian said.

Sienna pulled at her bottom lip. "Sure."

"I'll go get him. And since they only want one visitor at a time, I'll wait outside. Riley and I will drive you home when you're released." Ian placed a hand on her arm and squeezed for reassurance.

"Thanks, Ian."

"No problem." He walked out and she braced herself to see Ethan.

✧   ✧   ✧

AS SOON AS Ian walked back into the waiting room, Ethan stood up and strode over.

"She's fine. Good." Ian's easy smile reassured Ethan.

"If you want to go back, no one's in there with her now. I think they are just waiting for the doctor to sign off on her release." Ian gestured toward the double doors he'd come through.

"Ian?" Riley walked up to them, her cell phone in hand. "Sick kid at home. I've got to go."

"I came with the ambulance. I was going to drop Sienna off when she was released." Ian rolled his shoulders, obviously trying to figure out what to do.

"I've got it," Ethan said, the words tumbling out before he could censor them. "I'll wait around and drive her home."

Ian shot him a grateful look. "You sure?"

Ethan waved away the other man's concern. And that's how he ended up walking back to Sienna's cubicle, responsible for seeing her home safely now that her family was gone.

He approached the curtain. "Knock knock," he

said because there was no door.

"Come in."

He pushed back the curtain and walked into the small area. Sienna lay in a hospital bed, her dark hair falling around her face. A saline IV dripped into her and a blood pressure cuff was around her forearm. He didn't like how pale and fragile she looked or the memories it brought back, seeing her like this.

"Hey." He forced a smile.

She smiled at him. "Hi."

"How are you feeling?" he asked.

"Better."

He nodded, pulling up a chair and taking a seat beside the bed. "So apparently I'm your ride home. One of Ian and Riley's kids is sick and they had to go."

Her eyes opened wide. "You really don't need to stick around. I can–"

"If you say call an Uber, we're going to have a definite problem."

A cute blush stained her cheeks, and the fact that she had color back in her skin made him feel better.

"Okay. Thank you," she agreed, giving in.

"So." He didn't know how to broach the subject but he wanted to know more. He wanted to know everything about Sienna Dare. "Childhood leukemia, huh?"

She ducked her head and groaned. "Stupid family.

Big mouths, all of them. Who was it?" she asked.

"Unimportant." He wasn't about to throw Ian under the bus. "It came up by way of explaining why your entire family showed up in the waiting room, every one of them in a panic, worried about you."

She sighed. "I hate being the focus of all that attention. It's like when I was sick. Everyone worried about me when it was because of me that the entire family was thrown into turmoil. I didn't understand it when I was that young, but as I grew up, I found out. My father went to his first wife and told her he needed to have his kids tested for a bone marrow transplant for me. His illegitimate kid." She picked at the fabric on the blanket covering her. "I was the reason for the fallout. The divorce. Ian's hatred of us for years."

Ethan shook his head. "I hate to tell you this, but your father was the reason, honey. Not you." The term of endearment slipped out of his lips. Damned if it didn't feel right.

She swallowed hard. "Yes and no. But we can agree to disagree on that. I just hate being the cause of drama and discord."

He frowned, not liking how much weight she put on her slender shoulders.

"Avery donated her bone marrow. She ended up with severe anxiety attacks she has until this day because the news about my father came out. Florida hotel magnate with two families. People went nuts. The press followed him around and caught her and her mom coming out of the hospital. Flashing light bulbs, people screaming at her. She was never the same."

He reached over and took her hand. "Still not your fault." He hesitated, then asked, "Where was your father today?" By Ethan's count, every sibling she'd mentioned the other day had been in that waiting room. So had her mother.

"Umm … I don't know? Something's been going on with him. He hasn't been around as much and Mom won't talk about it. I definitely think my brothers know. I'm not sure about the girls, though Avery changes the subject whenever I mention it so…"

Ethan narrowed his gaze. Robert Dare sounded like a first-class asshole. "My father was and is a jerk."

She glanced at him, obviously startled he was sharing anything about himself with her at all. He just didn't want her to feel so isolated and alone. "When I was nineteen, my mom died of cancer. Dad fell apart. I mean, he was never the best father, and in Sebastian's case, he threw money at any problem, assuming he could make it go away. What Sebastian really needed was a kick in the ass and a father."

Ethan shook his head at the painful memories. "I did what I could for all my siblings. I dropped out of

Duke University and went to school in New York so I could be home. And Dad? He went from wife to wife. He's on number four now. Candy." He smiled wryly. "She's a shallow, attention-seeking–" He cut himself off before he could finish. "She wore white to Sierra's wedding." The word *whore* was what he thought of his stepmother, but she was his father's problem, not his.

He glanced at Sienna, who looked at him, eyes wide, mouth open. "I think those are the most words you've said to me since we met."

He couldn't hold back a laugh. It sounded rusty, and even Sienna appeared startled, making him realize how long it had been since anyone around him had penetrated the walls he'd built. Not even his siblings had been able to get through to him. Just this woman who pulled at things inside him he had wanted to shut down and lock up tight.

He cleared his throat. "I just wanted you to see that parents can be assholes. It doesn't make their actions your fault. You need to deal with that," he told her.

"Do you know what it's like to realize that every one of your siblings' issues – and I have a lot of siblings – stems from the fact that I got sick? If that secret remained–"

"Trust me, secrets never stay buried, and when they come out, they tend to do a hell of a lot of

112

damage."

He caught Sienna's stricken look but what could he say? He'd revealed enough about himself for one day. Mandy and everything he'd discovered since she'd died? Yeah, that didn't need to come out now.

"In your case, it can't be good for you to carry everyone's burden around," he said.

As if he had a right to counsel anyone on dealing with anything.

"Okay, I have your release papers, Ms. Dare. I just need to go over your instructions and we can let you go." The doctor peeked his head through the curtain.

Sienna glanced at Ethan, a slightly panicked look on her face. One he took to mean she wanted privacy for any discussion with her doctor, to which she was entitled, he thought.

"I'll go get the car and pull it up to the exit."

She visibly relaxed. "Thank you, Ethan." From the intense look in her eyes, he knew she appreciated more than just the ride.

The fact that he'd opened up to her was as shocking to him as it was to her. Something he needed to think about, process, and understand.

ETHAN STOOD IN the Miami apartment that Ian Dare had set him up in, a company place much like where he'd put Sienna when she'd been in New York. Glass of scotch in hand, he glanced at the lights twinkling down on the busy street below, where clubs played loud music and people who were much younger than him in truth and in their souls waited in lines to get inside.

He'd been in Miami twenty-four hours, and he already felt like he was changing. Opening up. Lightening up. All because of one woman.

He took a needed sip of his drink, his mind still on Sienna and what he was learning about her. She was sweeter than his wife had been, cared more for other people and even less about her own needs than her family's needs. Unlike Mandy, who'd wanted Ethan's attention and sole focus, and when she'd lost that, she'd gone looking elsewhere.

Thinking back, they'd been a solid couple in the beginning. A smart match as far as her working at KTT was concerned. But she put her own needs first, worrying more about herself than she did about him or their marriage. And sadly, he hadn't even been aware that things had gone south. He'd loved her, but had he been head over heels? Was she all he could think about? Had he been unable to keep his hands off her?

No.

Which was where his feelings for Sienna already

differed.

But Sienna had made her choices clear, and she wasn't interested in what he could or was willing to give. A clandestine affair. It sounded ugly now, even to his jaded ears. Because even he wanted more than that from her.

Yet he wanted to take care of Sienna, to know she was healthy and feeling good. When she'd fainted in his arms, his brain had spun into the past and fear had consumed him. Discovering she had had leukemia had definitely upset his equilibrium. The idea of losing her was not acceptable to him. She'd already gotten under his skin in ways not even Mandy ever had. He couldn't just ignore her, nor did he want to.

But he needed to be careful. He didn't want to insult her, didn't want her hurt, but he couldn't offer her more than what he'd proposed the other night. Despite wanting her desperately, he could not risk the business relationship with Ian Dare, and worse, he didn't want to give her the wrong impression.

That he was available. Which meant he had no alternative but to respect her wishes and keep his distance. No more seduction. No more sex. No more getting-to-know-her time.

He frowned and finished off the amber liquid, then poured himself more. He needed the fortitude to stay away from the alluring young woman who was beginning to consume his thoughts and his desires.

✧   ✧   ✧

SIENNA MADE SURE to do as the doctor instructed in his discharge orders. Rest when she could, keep herself hydrated, and eat small but frequent meals in an effort to maintain her blood pressure at normal levels. Unfortunately, he couldn't guarantee her she wouldn't faint again, and for sure the nausea wasn't going away.

Still, she managed to power through the workweek with no one the wiser. Only Olivia, with whom she basically shared an office, gave her funny looks when she occasionally ran to the ladies' room and returned looking paler and drinking a ginger ale. Sienna also didn't think she did a good job of hiding the saltines she kept in her purse and munched on when she could.

As for Ethan, she did her best to keep her distance except for business. They'd rescheduled the meeting with his team and the app developer, and that had gone well, Sienna managing to act like her normal, cheerful self throughout.

And Ethan kept the respectful distance that she'd insisted on but hated at the same time. She often caught him watching her, though, eyeing her with concern when they passed in the hall, almost as if he was waiting for her to faint again. But so far so good, and if she wished for more between them, wishing was all she'd let herself do.

He might be interested in sex, and she might want the same, but she had too much self-respect to fall into the same trap her mother had been in, hidden away from the outside world. Maybe Ethan Knight wasn't currently married, but he wasn't available to her in the ways that she both needed and wanted. Too soon, she'd have to let him know he was going to be a father and accept less than she wanted out of her role in his life, as it was. At the very least, she intended to keep her dignity.

"Sienna?"

"Yes?" She glanced up at Olivia, who sat on the corner of her desk, waiting to catch her attention.

"I'm starving. Want to go get some Mexican food? I could kill for a quesadilla. Gooey cheese, chicken, and oh! Maybe some guacamole, too."

At the too vivid description, her stomach churned uneasily. Dammit. "Umm … I'm not really in the mood for Mexican food." She braced her hand against her stomach and forced herself to take deep, easy breaths.

"Okay, what gives? You've been acting strangely all week. I get that you fainted, but you're still nauseous, I know you've gotten sick, and don't think I missed those crackers you have stashed in your purse." Olivia swung her foot back and forth from her perch on the desk. "If I didn't know better, I'd think you were pregnant."

The blood drained from Sienna's head. The one thing she couldn't do was outright lie to her half sister. "I…"

"I knew it. You *are* pregnant!" Olivia spoke too loudly, but it wouldn't have mattered if she'd kept a level tone of voice, because Ian chose that moment to show up in the open doorway.

"Repeat that one more time?" he said in a deadly sounding voice.

"Oh shit. Ian, that wasn't meant for you to hear." Olivia jumped up from her seat while Sienna scrambled for an explanation. "Sienna, I'm sorry."

She couldn't worry about Olivia now, not when Ian stood over her waiting for an answer. "I'm not pregnant … I mean, I am but…" Her words trailed off.

Why was it her half brother could merely act like the caveman scary man they feared while simultaneously projecting the fact that he was the caring parent they all needed and they caved, revealing information that never should have been made public?

"That's what the fainting spell was all about?" he asked, holding on to his famous temper.

She nodded. "But I'm fine. Really."

"Who's the father?" he asked, his tone low and steady, but she could see the throbbing at his temple and knew he was upset and concerned.

"None of your business," Olivia said, pulling at Ian's arm. "Back off, big brother."

He shot Olivia a glare. "While that may be true, I'm going to ask again." He met Sienna's gaze. "Because I care about you and it matters. Who is the father?"

She swallowed hard. She didn't have to tell him. She didn't owe him answers. But she also knew Ian well enough to understand he wouldn't let this go. Somehow he'd dig and dig until he discovered the truth anyway.

Secrets are bad, honey. We all know this firsthand. Her mother's words came back to her.

"It's Ethan Knight," she said, closing her eyes as the words escaped. "And he's going to hear it from me, not you." She jumped up from her seat, but Ian was faster, his long legs taking him out of the office quicker than she'd thought possible.

She glanced at Olivia. "Help me."

Together they ran after Ian, but from the yelling in the hall, they were too late.

ETHAN HUNG UP the phone with Sebastian, happy to

hear his brother and Ashley were talking about having a family in a way that meant Sebastian was open to the possibility, no longer shutting Ashley out because of his fears of repeating their father's mistakes.

Next he planned to walk the construction area with the foreman. He needed to make sure the schematics worked with the security keys. He didn't want a repeat of the California debacle with Keystone. The keys KTT installed weren't physical, per se, but used via a smartphone or special key configured to wirelessly perform the opening and closing process of any door in the stadium. But there were also mechanical parts, and those had been what Mandy had purchased substandard. Ethan wanted to see the parts for himself firsthand this time.

He rose from his seat in time to see Ian burst into his office, with what could only be described as rage contorting his face.

"Ian, what—"

"I sent my sister to you to look after and protect, and what do you do? Knock her up?" Ian let his right fist fly before Ethan could even process the other man's words, taking the hit and falling against the wall.

Head ringing, he forced himself to a standing position. "What the hell?"

"Sienna's pregnant and you're the father."

Ethan's hand went to his jaw, which hurt like a

motherfucker, the reason for Ian's anger just now penetrating. "Sienna is pregnant?"

Ian raised his fist again but Ethan caught the man's wrist in his hand. "You get one shot. You took it." He met Ian's furious stare. "Because I have a sister, I'm going to let that go." He drew a deep breath. "And for the record, I didn't know."

"And that makes it okay?" Ian shook his hand free of Ethan's grip.

"Ian, back off!" Sienna ran in, Olivia behind her, just as Ian pulled his arm away, and she grabbed for her brother. "Leave him alone!"

Heart firing in his chest, Ethan drew a deep breath, his gaze on Sienna's. Her eyes were wide, her face pale, her entire body shaking with fear.

He wanted to wrap her up in his arms and protect her. He also wanted to run far and fast. "We need to talk," he said gruffly.

"You're off the project, Knight. Pack up your things and get the fuck out," Ian said.

Sienna narrowed her gaze. "This is exactly what I didn't want to happen!" she shouted.

Both men's gaze turned her way. "I'm sick and tired of being the center of drama, whether it's two families or a business," she said tiredly. "Ian, this is between Ethan and me. Not you."

Her sibling narrowed his gaze. "This discussion

isn't over but your role in the stadium is." He stormed out of the room, Olivia rushing after him, clearly hoping to calm him down.

Good luck, he thought to himself. If Ethan sent his sister to Miami and some older asshole had knocked her up, Ethan would be beyond furious. So yeah, he'd cut Dare some slack. But not too much, because as Sienna had said, this was none of his business.

This being a baby.

Holy fucking shit.

Ethan's jaw stung and his head pounded, his mind reeling at the truth now staring him in the face. Sienna was pregnant with his baby.

He turned to her. She looked very frail and extremely anxious as she faced him.

"That's why you fainted?" he asked.

She nodded, guiltily.

"And you didn't tell me because…? Are you not planning on keeping it?" Nausea filled him at the thought.

"Oh my God, no." She sounded horrified at the suggestion that she might abort their child. "I mean, everyone has to make their own choices, but that never entered my mind."

The knot that had formed in his gut suddenly eased. He might not have planned for this, he might not have wanted it, but she was carrying a part of him. He was relieved she hadn't thought about not keeping it.

"Then why didn't you tell me?" he asked, pulling out a chair and easing her into it.

She narrowed her gaze, clearly not liking him fussing over her. "Because of what just happened! I knew Ian would have a fit and I knew the stadium contract was important to you both. You made it pretty damned clear the other night just how you prioritized things. I didn't want to get in the way."

It was his turn to wince because he'd done just that. Told her the stadium was more important than any kind of relationship they could have. He'd devalued her, something he was coming to see more and more as time went on and things around him unraveled.

But she'd known about the baby for almost a week. "So you were never going to tell me? Just let me go home and not know I had a kid?" He ground his teeth together, harder when she rolled her eyes at him.

"Of course not. I was just waiting until you'd finished your company's work on the stadium. I wanted it to be too late for Ian to hurt your business. Which he now has." Her brother had made it perfectly clear where things stood between the Thunder Stadium and KTT.

Jesus. Leave it to Sienna to try and protect him despite how shitty he'd treated her.

Pregnant. The word rattled around in his brain and he ran a hand through his hair and groaned. "I don't fucking believe this."

Although he really could. He vividly remembered waking up that morning in New York, his body wrapped around Sienna's, his mind half-asleep as he thrust his hard cock inside her wet heat. He thought he'd come to himself in enough time to pull out and keep her safe from pregnancy but clearly not. Nature had other plans.

"It was as much a shock to me as it is to you." Her voice grew soft. "I was told I probably would never be able to get pregnant... after the chemo and the treatment." She rolled her shoulders, her hand coming to rest on her stomach protectively. "This is a miracle for me."

His gaze jerked to hers, the import of that statement settling into his bones. God, the things this woman had endured throughout her life. Childhood leukemia, vicious treatments, her family's unraveling, thinking she'd never have children of her own if she wanted them. She was stronger than anyone he'd ever met, himself included, and he admired the hell out of her.

"We'll figure things out," he said, unsure of what

else to say at the moment. He was still coming to terms with something she'd had a week to accept.

She nodded. "I don't expect anything from you ... when it comes to me, I mean. Because I think deep down you're a good man, I'm assuming you'll want to have a role in this baby's life and I want that, too."

Her eyes grew damp but she stood up straight, remaining strong in front of him. "But you've been perfectly up-front with me about where we stand. I don't want you worrying you're going to have some clingy woman demanding you step up and marry her." Her self-deprecating smile tugged at his heart.

Dammit, he was coming to hate himself more and more.

"Sienna—"

She shook her head. "I have to go. I have work to do." She stood up and walked out, leaving him alone in his assigned office, reeling.

Chapter Seven

SIENNA SAT ON her sofa, legs crossed, sipping a decaffeinated iced tea, the book *What to Expect When You're Expecting* open on her coffee table, on her laptop, articles on cancer patients carrying babies to term on her browser. She had an appointment with an ob-gyn next week, one who specialized in high-risk pregnancies. Just in case.

And she tried to focus on the tiny nugget inside her belly and not the state of her life since Ian had found out and taken a swing at Ethan. Because Olivia had called and told her that Ethan was gone. He'd taken a late flight out of Miami, back to New York. Upset didn't begin to describe how she felt, but she had no choice but to accept his decision to leave.

And blame Ian.

Which was why she jumped up from her sitting position, pulled on a summer dress and flip-flops, and headed in her car to see Ian at his home with his wife and kids. Sienna loved Ian and Riley's kids. Rainey was an adorable four-year-old with brown wavy hair like her mother and a handful, which, as far as Sienna was concerned, served Ian right. Of course he smothered and doted on his daughter, who had no problem telling her daddy what she wanted. Jack was almost a year old and the spitting image of his father. Another male Dare to dominate the world, Sienna thought wryly.

And since she loved Ian's wife and knew Riley would take her side when it came to Ian's interference in Sienna's life, she had no problem tackling the problem in his home. After all, this was Sienna's personal life she was dealing with.

She drove the twenty minutes outside of Miami to the house Ian had bought after moving out of his downtown condo in the Ritz and pulled up to her brother's close to eight p.m. She'd expected the kids would be asleep, although she was both surprised and thrilled to find them awake.

No sooner had Riley let her into the house than Rainey, in her nightgown and wild hair, came bursting into the room. "Aunt Sienna! Let's play dolls!"

Riley, looking tired, glanced at her daughter and sighed. "She napped after four p.m. Needless to say, sleep is not on the agenda."

"Go get your American Girl," Sienna said of Rainey's favorite toy, and the little girl disappeared, running for her room.

Riley ushered her inside. "I don't know why you're here but you're a godsend. I need help."

Sienna laughed. "I came to yell at my brother, but hanging out with my niece is always a treat."

"I'm back!" Rainey yelled her words. She grasped Sienna's hand and pulled her into the family room, placing the doll in Sienna's lap. The doll was intended to look just like Rainey and it did, from the nightgown to her currently unbrushed hair.

"Uh-oh. What did Ian do now?" Riley joined her in the room with the large sofa and glanced at Sienna.

She gave Ian's wife a quick explanation that included whispers so Rainey didn't overhear. "Long story short, it's none of his business what goes on between Ethan and me."

"You're right about that!" Riley's eyes had opened wide, an annoyed expression on her face. "And you're pregnant!" Riley exclaimed, pulling her into a hug. "No wonder Ian was in such an ornery mood tonight. He said we'd talk after the kids went to bed. I bet he knew I'd be furious and he was delaying the inevitable showdown."

Sienna shrugged. "Wouldn't surprise me. But I need to make things clear to him about boundaries, you know?"

Riley nodded. "I certainly do."

Ian and Riley had had their own issues getting together, ones that involved Ian's domineering ways.

"He's putting Jack to bed. He'll be back down in a few minutes," she said.

Sienna sat down next to Rainey and accepted the doll. "Now, what can we do with … what's your doll's name?" Sienna knew Rainey changed the doll's name on a whim.

"Gracie!" the little girl exclaimed and Riley's eyes opened wide.

"Rainey, have you been sneaking around, listening when Mommy and Daddy are talking again?" Riley asked her daughter, trying to keep a stern voice.

She looked up with big violet eyes that resembled her father's. The rest of her was all Riley. "Maybe, Mommy."

Sienna choked on the answer. "Maybe?"

"Rainey Noelle, what does that mean?" Riley placed a hand under her daughter's chin and forced her to meet her gaze.

"You told me not to lie, so I'm not, Mommy."

"Are you sure she's only four?" Sienna grinned at the little girl.

Riley leaned back against the sofa cushion. "She's a Dare. She's her father's daughter. And she's smarter than she should be."

"So you heard that Daddy and I want to name your new baby sister Gracie?" Riley asked through a half smile.

Sienna whipped her head around to Riley. "You're having another girl?"

Riley nodded. "It was supposed to be a secret." She shook her head and sighed.

"Just like my baby was supposed to be a secret. Then Ian found out and ran right to the father."

"Of course I did. The man had to know that he violated my trust." Ian strode into the room.

He'd changed from the suit he wore to the office and had on a pair of black track pants and a tee shirt with what looked like marinara stains. Nobody would believe this was the same formidable Ian Dare people ran away from in fear.

Riley rose to her feet. "I'm going to take Rainey for a bath. Maybe that will calm her down and make her want to go to sleep. Honey, say good night to your Aunt Sienna."

"Night, Aunt Sienna!" Rainey hugged Sienna tight, and at the feel of her little arms squeezing her, a lump formed in Sienna's throat.

She was having a baby, something she'd never, ever thought was possible. She hadn't even let herself contemplate alternatives to normal childbirth. She hadn't been at the right stage of her life for that. But now that she was pregnant, the reality was hitting her. This would be her life but she'd be doing it alone. She squared her shoulders, knowing she would handle anything life threw her way. She already had.

"Night, honey." Sienna kissed the top of Rainey's head.

Riley took her daughter's hand. "Ian, you should know I agree with Sienna and we're going to have a long talk tonight."

He winced, something Ian would only do when his wife was angry with him.

Riley walked out with Rainey, the little girl chatting about her bath and her toys.

Ian waited until they were alone before turning to her. "You're furious."

Sienna stood. "That's putting it mildly, Ian. You told Ethan he was the father before I was ready. Then you sent him away, firing him from a job that means the world to you both. And you hit him!"

Ian ran a hand over his face and groaned. "I can guarantee you if I'd done to his sister what he did to you, Ethan would have reacted exactly the same way."

"That doesn't make it right!" She paced the floor in Ian's family room. "You need to understand that this is my life. I'm the one who hooked up with Ethan and got pregnant, and I have to deal with the conse-quences, including the father of my baby! You can't run him off. Where does that leave me?"

She imagined Ethan was taking the weekend to

come to terms with the news she'd already had time to digest. What would happen after that was anybody's guess, but she knew he wouldn't be returning to the stadium.

"It was disrespectful of him to take advantage of you, but you're right. It's your life. Your choices. I'm sorry."

Ignoring the *it was disrespectful* comment, because she had no intention of telling Ian she had propositioned Ethan, she focused on the more important part of Ian's statement. And nearly reeled in shock. "Excuse me, what did you say?"

An amused smile pulled at his mouth. "I said I'm sorry. It's one of those things Riley has taught me. To apologize when I'm wrong."

She placed her hands on her hips and eyed him warily. "What's the catch?"

"I'm sorry I screwed things up for you. I'm not sorry I told Ethan how I felt and I'm sure he respects me for it." Ian grinned unrepentantly.

"Fat lot of good that does me with him gone," Sienna muttered.

Ian placed his hand on her back and pulled her into him. "If he's half the man I think he is, he'll be back."

She rolled her eyes. Ian Dare was so frustratingly dense. Then again, maybe he was right. She wouldn't

133

know until she heard from Ethan and they talked again.

"You're going to be okay," Ian said. "You have the best support system there is and more aunts and uncles than your baby will know what to do with."

She smiled. That much, at least, she knew to be true. She stepped back and looked up at her half brother. "Do we have an understanding, though? You'll stay out of my personal life?"

"You're going to want me around when the baby is born," he said smugly.

"I'll take that as a yes." It was the best she was going to get from him, she knew.

✧　✧　✧

STANDING IN HIS apartment in Manhattan, Ethan felt like he'd been gone a month instead of the week he'd been in Miami. In fact, if he didn't know better, he'd say he'd become an entirely different man. Sure as fuck, he was going to be a father.

He ran his hand through his hair, shocked when a knock sounded on his door. Nobody knew he was back in town. He purposely hadn't told anyone, wanting time alone to process what had gone down and decide how he was going to handle things going forward. He walked over and opened the door to find Sebastian on the other side.

"John told me you were back," Sebastian said of the doorman as he strode past Ethan without waiting to be invited in. "Any reason I didn't know?"

"Because I needed time alone," Ethan said pointedly.

Sebastian sat down on the sofa in the family room, deliberately not taking the hint. "Talk to me, Ethan. Last time I saw you, I found out you'd slept with Ian's sister. Now you're home out of the blue. Why?"

"You wouldn't believe me if I told you." He settled into his favorite club chair across from his brother.

"You fucked her again?"

An unwilling smile tipped Ethan's mouth. "I tried."

Sebastian raised his eyebrows. "She turned you down?"

"And threw a salt shaker at me."

His brother burst out laughing. "I think I like this woman. At the very least, she challenges you."

"That's putting it mildly." Ethan clasped his hands together and met his brother's gaze. "I asked her to have an affair and keep it a secret."

Sebastian shook his head. "Oh, brother. You are a piece of work."

"How the hell was I supposed to know her father kept her mother a dirty secret for years?"

Leaning forward, Sebastian rested on his elbows.

"And you think that's the only reason that was the wrong move?"

Ethan rose to his feet, unable to sit still. "No. It was a shitty thing to do. In my defense, I was trying to protect the stadium contract." Which, he still had to tell his brother, was in jeopardy.

He walked over to the window and glanced out at the nighttime sky, feeling small in comparison, which was ironic because his problems felt huge.

"What's really going on?" Sebastian's voice interrupted his thoughts.

Ethan drew a deep breath and turned to face him. "Sienna is pregnant."

Sebastian's eyes opened wide. "And you're sure you're the father?"

"Yes." No need to share that Sienna had been a virgin. Some things ought to stay private, and the fact that she'd chosen him to give herself to first was one of them.

"Christ, you don't do things halfway, do you?"

Might as well give him the rest of it, Ethan thought. "Ian found out and threw me out." Shoving his hands into his front pants pockets, Ethan kicked at the floor.

Ian's punch still grated but he wasn't about to go after Sienna's brother. Not when Ethan had deserved at least one solid shot.

"You do realize we have a binding contract with the Thunder? That he can't terminate the contract because you knocked up his sister?" Sebastian asked.

Ethan nodded. "Yeah. I know." Once he'd calmed down, it was one of the first things he'd realized. "I just wanted to give everyone a chance to chill before I pushed my way back in there."

"And the baby? What are your plans there? Because when I told you that Ashley wanted a family, your exact words were, *better you than me.*"

Ethan winced. "I felt that way. I still sort of feel that way. I mean, I barely have my head out of my ass when it comes to what Mandy did to me. Now I'm going to have a baby?" Panic rushed through him at the thought, but at the same time, so did a flicker of excitement he couldn't contain.

"Hey." Sebastian put a hand on Ethan's shoulder. "Let's back up, okay? First, can I get you a drink?"

Ethan nodded.

After walking over to the bar, Sebastian poured them both tumblers of whiskey, handing one to Ethan.

He took a long sip and groaned at the burn as the liquid went down.

Sebastian did the same. "Aaah," he said, shaking his head after the drink. "How do you feel about Sienna? Why don't we start there?"

How did he feel about Sienna? He'd been trying to

avoid that very question since the moment he'd laid eyes on her. Something about her had drawn him from the beginning and not just her looks, although there was her innocent beauty that called to him. But her outgoing personality, her pure joy in any situation, and the way she rolled with the punches, taking what life threw at her with seeming ease. Even when it hadn't been fair.

And life hadn't been fucking fair to her, that much he knew. Still, she loved it. Loved her family, her new job... Did he want her to love him? Maybe it was too soon for that, but he wanted a lot more from her than he'd been willing to admit so far.

"She makes me feel again," he said slowly, finding it difficult to come up with the right words to answer Sebastian's question. "At first it was uncomfortable as hell, but I didn't have to worry about it because it was one weekend and done." He paced the floor in the room and Sebastian sipped his drink, letting Ethan deal with things in his own way.

"After Mandy died, I thought life was over. Then blow after blow came and I figured it really couldn't get much worse." He finished his drink in one long gulp and placed the glass on the nearest coffee table. "And then this young woman blows into my life and gives me a weekend to remember. Next thing I know, I'm seeing her again in Miami and I can't stay away."

He saw his brother's grin and ignored it, not wanting to deal with sibling teasing and shit right now. Being smart, Sebastian seemed to sense Ethan's need to be serious and talk this through.

"I want her but I feel protective of her at the same time. She's strong despite being dealt a shitty hand in life and I don't mean just her asshole father."

Sebastian, remaining silent, raised an eyebrow.

"Childhood leukemia. She didn't even think she could get pregnant. And then she passed out on me and my heart just about fell to my feet. After I got over the fact that this wasn't an overdose like Mandy, all I wanted to do was bundle her up and keep her safe, but she was barely talking to me at this point. Next thing I know, Ian's taking a swing at me for knocking up his sister."

Wincing, Sebastian asked, "Did you hit him back?"

Ethan chuckled. "Hell no. If he'd gotten Sierra pregnant, I'd have belted him, too. I gave him one shot. Then he threw me out."

"And you just left her?" Sebastian's mouth opened wide, his jaw hanging in shock.

"Not exactly." Ethan shrugged. "We talked but I didn't tell her I was leaving. One of her sisters saw me go and asked what my plans were, so I'm sure Sienna knows."

With a groan, Sebastian sat back down on the sofa

and kicked his feet up on the table. "Man, you know how to get in deep. So what's next? I know you're not blowing this deal, so once you lay out the situation for Ian, what are you doing about the baby? Is there a wedding in the future?"

For all the times Ethan had been the parent to his siblings, he'd never been on the receiving end quite like this.

He closed his eyes, not wanting to see the disappointment in Sebastian's gaze when he told him the rest. "Sienna said she didn't expect anything from me." And that had hurt badly.

"Okay then. Child support only it is."

"Fuck no!" Ethan said, offended his brother would think *that* little of him. "I'm not abandoning the baby or the mother of my child."

"Well, is that all she is to you? You said she makes you feel, but what do you want from her?"

Ethan pulled at his hair before turning on his brother. "Fuck you, Dr. Freud. Are you finished pounding me with questions?"

"Just trying to get you to see all the angles," his brother said too helpfully.

If Ethan wasn't mistaken, Sebastian was enjoying Ethan's unraveling. He forced himself to look deep inside himself and think about the fair question.

"I want her. I want her in my life. And I want to

see where this thing between us can go." Because she brought him joy where he'd had none. She made him smile. She made him want to step up and be the guy who she admired, not the asshole who asked her to stay hidden. "And not because she's pregnant with my child."

Sebastian placed his hands behind his head and leaned back against the sofa, a gleam in his eye. "Then I guess you have your work cut out for you, don't you?"

"No fucking kidding," Ethan muttered to himself, his mind already whirling with ideas about what he could do to romance Sienna and convince her she meant more to him than he'd shown her so far.

Not the way he'd expected his life to go. Then again, very little in the last couple of years had been what he'd anticipated. With some due diligence and planning, just maybe he could turn things around and make them work out for a change.

MONDAY MORNING, ETHAN walked into the stadium like he had every right to be there and headed directly to Ian's office. He arrived early because he knew the other man did the same, and if at all possible, he wanted to avoid Sienna witnessing another confrontation between him and her brother. He even got there before Ian's secretary, which enabled him to take the other man by surprise.

He knocked once and walked into Ian's office, coming to a stop when Ian rose from his desk.

"I didn't think I'd get rid of you that easily," Ian muttered.

"No. I went home for the weekend to get my head on straight and give you time to cool off."

"And if I haven't?" Ian folded his arms across his chest, defiant and still pissed off.

"Ask me if I give a shit," Ethan muttered. "Look, I respect you both as a businessman and as Sienna's brother, but the fact is, what goes on between her and me has nothing to do with you."

The other man frowned. "She paid me a visit Friday night and said pretty much the same thing. Then my wife laid into me when Sienna left and I'm lucky I didn't sleep on the couch."

As much as Ethan didn't like the idea of Sienna getting worked up confronting Ian, he appreciated the fact that she went to bat for him. For them. Not that she knew there was a them yet, but that would come.

"As far as the stadium contract," Ethan continued, wanting to make all his points before Ian could gather his own thoughts, "legally you can't throw my company off the project. You don't have a leg to stand on, so I'm back and we're working together."

Ian's scowl deepened.

The one thing Ethan didn't want to do was be on opposing sides with Sienna's brother, so he stepped forward. "Look, for Sienna's sake, I want us to get along. And I'll even admit that I don't blame you one bit for how you're feeling. But you can't change things. It is what it is and she's my responsibility now."

If Ethan was being honest with himself, he'd wanted that job ever since Sienna had given him her sweet little body and surprised him with her virginity. Did it make him a possessive alpha-male asshole? You bet it did. Did he care? Not in the least.

The only part that sucked in all this was how long it had taken him to get his head on straight and realize what he wanted. Now she was pregnant, and though he was grateful it had shown him the light, he knew damn well she'd believe his turnaround was all because of the baby.

Like Sebastian had said, Ethan had his work cut out for him. But he had every intention of showing her he was a better man with her in his life. He might not deserve her but he wasn't letting her go. He just didn't need her brother standing in the way.

Ian burst out laughing, taking Ethan by surprise. "You think she's yours to take care of? She's as independent as they come, and you've done nothing to show her she means jack shit to you. At least not that

I've seen, so good luck, asshole." Ian sat back down at his desk, picking up papers, effectively dismissing Ethan.

Oddly enough, Ethan wasn't insulted and this meeting had gone better than he'd hoped. He had a lot in common with Ian Dare and could see his side of things completely. Just recently, his sister's wedding had been derailed by her ex-boyfriend objecting at the service, then stealing Sierra away for a long weekend to convince her to take him back. Ethan had wanted nothing more than to throttle Ryder Hammond, but Parker and Sebastian had kept Ethan calm and he'd let fate play out. Sierra was now happily married to Ryder and pregnant with his baby.

Ethan just wanted Ian to back the hell off the same way. Convinced he'd done all he could on this end, he strode out of Ian's office and headed to the one assigned to him. Since Ian had thrown his ass out on Friday, nobody had had time to clean out his space, which meant he could pick up where he'd left off.

Sitting down at his desk, he pulled open his laptop and got to work.

✦ ✦ ✦

AFTER IAN HAD hit Ethan and thrown him off the project, the office had buzzed in excitement. The reveal of Sienna's pregnancy thanks to her brother's big mouth had added to the gossiping. With Ethan gone, Sienna expected more of a quiet day today.

She sat at her desk munching on saltine crackers when she heard voices in the hallway.

"He's back," a woman said.

"Do you think Mr. Dare knows? Maybe he'll go after him again," another voice said.

And just like that, she knew Ethan had returned despite Ian's dictate. Her stomach fluttered at the notion and she deliberately tamped down on the excited feeling. He was back for the stadium. He wasn't going to give up a billion-dollar contract just because Ian had gotten his panties in a twist. He'd already made it clear to her how important this deal was to him.

With a frown, she bit down on the cracker hard, annoyed when all the crumbs fell on top of the pages she'd been reading about demographics and stats regarding fantasy football.

Olivia normally worked in the inner office, but she was out dealing with meetings today, which left Sienna alone with her thoughts. She buried herself in statistics and the morning passed quickly. Although she didn't seem to have the nausea under control, the vomiting and dizziness were, so she was able to go out and pick up lunch without worry.

She placed her hand on her desk, about to push

herself up when a shadow loomed over her. She knew immediately who it was.

Steeling herself, she glanced up into Ethan's blue eyes.

"Hey, beautiful."

She blinked, startled by both his presence and choice of words. "You're back." Well, that was brilliant, she thought, annoyed because he robbed her of the power of logical speech. Of course he was back. He was standing right in front of her.

He grinned, sitting his ass down on her desk. "I'm back and I want to talk to you."

"Okay?" They had issues they'd need to work out after the baby was born but nothing she could think of before then.

"First, have you had a doctor's appointment yet? For the baby?" he asked.

Her mouth grew dry as she shook her head. "No. It's tomorrow."

"What time? I'll take you," he said, not asked.

She narrowed her gaze. "Why?"

An amused smile lifted his lips. His sexy lips. Why was he suddenly so relaxed and at ease?

She was anything but.

"Because I want to be with you throughout this process." He glanced at her as if the answer was obvious, and she couldn't tear her gaze from his handsome face, hint of stubble, and full lips.

That nausea began to return. "Umm, okay, but it's really not necessary to come with me."

"Oh, but it is." His gaze darkened, his eyes narrowing, letting her know he meant it.

She blew out a breath. "Okay, tomorrow, ten a.m." If she wanted to ditch him, she could skip work and go straight from home.

It's not like he knew who her doctor was or where she was located. She just didn't see the need for him to be there.

"Are you going from the office or straight from your place?" he asked.

She pursed her lips, annoyed he'd out-thought her. "From home."

"Great." He smiled, obviously pleased. "I'll pick you up. How's nine thirty? Enough time?"

She nodded, knowing when to give in but not happy about his sudden need to join her.

"Don't look so annoyed. You need to get used to having me around. Now, about us."

This time the breath left her lungs. "What about us?" she managed to ask.

"I'd like to talk." He met her stare, his expression serious. "There's a lot you don't know about me, things that will explain my past behavior. Things you need to know."

At the thought of learning more about this enigmatic, sexy man, her heart beat hard in her chest, even as she warned herself discovering his secrets didn't mean anything between them had changed.

She slicked her tongue over her lower lip, aware that his gaze followed the movement, and a glance down at his waist showed her his body had reacted to her inadvertent gesture. Well, sexual desire had never been their issue.

"You can come by my place tonight," she said, ignoring the shakiness in her voice. "We can talk then." She hesitated, then decided to be both bold and honest. "But that's all we're going to do. There won't be a repeat of the other night." Her fingers curled into fists at her sides, her body aching for the repeat she was denying them. The hot sex he performed so well, the way their bodies danced in unison, so perfect as he slid into her.

"Message received," he said, disappointment in his eyes but understanding in his tone.

And she wasn't finished despite her traitorous body.

Straightening her shoulders, she dove into more dangerous territory. "And I meant what I said. I don't expect anything from you, so there's no need to come to doctor's appointments or hold my hand during this pregnancy. I'll give you access to the baby no matter what. I want my child to know you."

He leaned in so close his scent enveloped her and she became aware of his body heat. "*Our* child. And what if I want you to expect things from me?"

She shook her head hard, knowing better than to trust this sudden turnaround. He couldn't have gone from wanting to hide their relationship to wanting to flaunt it… unless it was all about the baby. Disappointment churned in her stomach at the thought, but this wasn't the time or the place to express her feelings or reveal her crazy emotions and hormones, which suddenly had her almost crying.

His lips were close to hers, his expression sad. "I didn't do right by you before. But I'm going to now." Reaching out, he fingered a strand of her long hair, and as impossible as it seemed, she felt that touch deep in her core.

Her pulse thundered and she wished he'd close the gap between them and kiss her, then berated herself for wanting something that was only going to mess with her heart even more.

The pad of his thumb stroked her cheek. "I'm going out to pick up lunch. Can I bring you back something?"

Food. He was offering her food. But his mouth was still so near and his breath was warm. She squirmed in her seat, unable to pull away.

"What are you getting to eat?" she asked, her voice suddenly hoarse.

"How about burgers? And milkshakes?"

Her gaze fell to the sexy shape of his lips, and she was tempted to initiate the kiss herself, but her stomach chose that moment to growl in reaction.

"Sounds like that's my cue." He laughed as he stood, breaking the intense connection between them.

She did her best not to blush, but she knew better than to think she could control the flush now staining her cheeks red with embarrassment.

"I'll be back with lunch."

"I'll be waiting." She held her breath until he walked out before laying her head down on the desk.

What was he doing to her, turning on the charm and turning up the heat between them? And how did she hope to resist him when she'd never been able to before?

Chapter Eight

E THAN ARRIVED AT Sienna's place with flowers in hand. He'd spent thirty minutes at the shop picking out just the right bouquet, ultimately choosing wildflowers to go with the spirit he sensed in Sienna.

"Thank you! I love them!" she said as he handed her the flowers. Her pleased smile told him he'd made the right choice. She put them in a vase with water and gave them a prominent place on the table in the family room.

Stomach churning at the prospect of what he was about to reveal to her, about his past, about himself, he waited for her to tell him where she wanted them to talk.

Ultimately, he followed her into the big room with the sofa and settled beside her.

She curled a leg beneath her, her knee touching his thigh. "So." She stared up at him wide-eyed, obviously eager to hear what he had to say.

"So." He didn't see any point in beating around the bush.

"I was married."

She sucked in a startled breath. "Was?" she asked, clearly needing the reassurance that when she'd been with him in New York, he was free and clear.

"Was. Mandy passed away from an accidental drug overdose about a year ago." The shock and pain of that moment, finding his wife cold on their bed, stayed with him to this day.

"Ethan, I'm so sorry," Sienna said, clutching his hand in hers.

He cleared his throat. "Mandy was an addict," he went on, curling his fingers around Sienna's for support. "And while she was in California overseeing a huge deal for KTT, she was buying substandard parts for a ridiculously high amount of money and pocketing the difference along with her dealer. Who, I might add, she was sleeping with." He blew out a harsh breath, admitting he'd been blindsided by his own wife.

Sienna blinked in obvious surprise. "She stole from your company and cheated on *you*? Was she insane?"

He chuckled at her words, appreciating the moral support.

Before he could speak, Sienna went on. "Addiction is a disease but the choices she made were her own. And if I were married to a man like you, nobody else would catch my eye," she said, blurting out her innermost feelings.

He jerked his gaze to hers, surprised she'd let him in that much, and from the bright flush on her cheeks, she'd shocked herself as well. Now wasn't the time to react to the sentiment but he tucked it away close to his heart.

"Mandy hurt me," he said, instead focusing on why he was giving Sienna so much personal information. "She fucked me up until my family no longer recognized me," he admitted. "And because she took me so off guard, she destroyed my belief in people. And she definitely stole any desire I had to move forward with a woman. Suffice it to say I wasn't prepared for you." He clenched his jaw, the admission pulled from him.

It wasn't easy to admit she affected him deeply.

Her self-deprecating smile disarmed him as she said, "I wasn't prepared for you, either."

He chuckled, ready to lighten the mood. "Most people aren't."

She leaned an elbow against the back cushion of the sofa. "Well, Ian Dare is my half brother. He didn't want anything to do with my part of the family after finding out about us. Trust me when I say if I can deal with him, I knew when I heard about you that I could handle you."

Ethan cocked his head to one side. This was the first he'd heard that she'd been warned about him.

"When you heard about me?"

"Sierra mentioned that you might be … difficult," she admitted. "But I wasn't worried."

And that was why he was so drawn to her. Where other people ran away, she ran toward him. "You blew me away with your openness and your inviting smile. And I couldn't stop staring at you because you were so fucking beautiful. I kept running through a list of reasons why I needed to keep my hands to myself, but I couldn't do it."

"Considering I propositioned you, I obviously couldn't stay away from you, either."

He knew that wasn't an invitation now. She'd made her feelings clear, but that didn't mean he wasn't going to show her what he wanted from her. He leaned in, close to those damp lips he wanted to suck into his mouth and taste.

She lifted a hand, placed her palm on his chest, and held him at bay. "Nope. Not happening." But her gaze flickered with disappointment, and he knew it wasn't any easier for her to keep her distance than it was for him.

But he'd hurt her and she clearly wasn't ready to open herself up to him again. Not that he blamed her. "I'll just continue with my apology, then."

"You were apologizing?" she teased him, her lips lifting in a grin.

"I was getting there." He paused, then said, "Here's the thing. During our weekend, what I felt for you, I've never experienced anything like it and it scared me. After what happened with Mandy? I didn't want to get involved with anyone ever again."

She nodded in understanding. "We're good, Ethan. I'm not the type to hold a grudge. We'll get through this pregnancy and co-parent like two adults."

He narrowed his gaze. "Is that what you took from this conversation? Because I want more, Sienna. I want to be more than just two people who happen to share a baby."

"Something you decided after finding out I was pregnant." She braced her hands on her thighs and pushed herself to a standing position. "Forgive me if it feels too convenient."

He knew she was about to end the conversation and perhaps even ask him to leave. Rising, he strode over to her, tipped her head up with his finger, and asked, "What are you afraid of, Sienna Dare?"

"You already asked me to hide the relationship once, and though I completely understand why now, it doesn't take away the sting. And it's hard for me to believe you would have come to this decision without the baby as the reason."

He inclined his head, conceding her point. "Let's say the baby woke me up. Made me face my fears. Are you going to hold that against me?"

She blew out a long breath. "I have too many hormones running through my body for me to answer that," she said honestly.

"Fair enough." He took a step back, gratified by the disappointment in her gaze. She might be pushing him away, but she didn't like it when he complied with her request.

Good to know.

"I'll go. I've left you with enough to think about, but I'll be back at nine thirty tomorrow to take you to the doctor. Do you want to go get something to eat first?" he asked.

She shook her head. "Mornings are hard for me. I'm pretty nauseous and I can't eat until later in the day.

He hated hearing that she was suffering. "Okay. See you in the morning." He was tempted to kiss her but he didn't want to push his luck.

She was talking to him now and not throwing things. He'd take it as a win.

✧   ✧   ✧

SIENNA SAT IN the exam room at the ob-gyn. After she'd changed into a gown, she'd texted Ethan and told him he could come in. He'd been adamant about not wanting to miss anything and she couldn't deny his request. She was using Riley's doctor and she'd already gotten her records from her general practitioner, who was well-versed in her past. Despite her frustration, Ian had had Riley call and explain Sienna's situation, and at Dr. Finley's request, Sienna had faxed everything over ahead of time. Suffice it to say, the doctor was prepared for Sienna.

But Sienna wasn't prepared for Ethan's nervousness, his pacing, and his constant glances, as if he was afraid she'd pass out any second.

"Sit down," she said, frustrated with him. "I'm fine. I haven't had another fainting incident since I started eating every two hours. And just because we're at the doctor doesn't mean you need to lose your mind. You're going to make me crazy."

"Sorry," he muttered and lowered himself into the chair by the table where she sat. She had to admit it was kind of endearing the way he worried.

A knock sounded on the exam room door and a middle-age woman walked in with a large smile on her face. "Sienna Dare?"

"Hi." She instinctively placed her hand over her stomach, something she'd been doing more and more lately.

"And you are the baby's father, I assume?"

Ethan nodded, rising from his seat. "Ethan Knight."

"I'm Dr. Finley and it's nice to meet you both." She walked over to a computer screen and pulled up what Sienna assumed was her file. "So I've been through your records and before we start, I'd like to reassure you about a few things."

To her surprise, Ethan stepped over and clasped Sienna's hand in his. The comfort she took from both his touch and presence was immeasurable. Ethan's hand squeezed hers so hard she feared for her bones.

"Just because you had childhood leukemia, pregnancy does not raise the risk of your cancer coming back or your child getting the disease," the doctor said.

"Thank God." As if his legs gave out, Ethan practically fell back into the chair beside her, and her relief was as palpable as his. She'd been reading about these things all weekend, but to hear a professional say it made her feel so much better.

"We're going to monitor your heart and your vital organs extra carefully, but it's been so many years since your treatments that I'm not overly concerned. I just want you to be aware of anything unusual that you feel and don't feel funny calling me to ask." Dr. Finley smiled at them, and for the first time since finding out she was pregnant, Sienna found herself truly at ease.

"You have no idea how grateful I am that you started out with that," she told the doctor. "Now I can focus on the baby."

"And that is what we're going to do. My nurse will draw blood after I examine you. Normally we'd only do a sonogram if there was a question on your due date? As in, do you know when you conceived?"

Blushing, Sienna nodded.

"Oh, we're sure," Ethan said in a gruff voice. "Three weeks ago." He had risen again and stood by her side, a solid, calming presence.

The doctor chuckled. "Okay. Normally we wait until eight weeks for a sonogram, but given the circumstances, I'm going to do one now and calm everyone's nerves."

"Okay," Sienna said, her excitement building, at last.

The nurse rolled the machine into the room and the doctor readied everything including pulling up Sienna's gown and prepping her for a vaginal ultrasound, the only type they could do this early in the pregnancy. She glanced at Ethan.

His gaze was on hers, his eyes warm. She couldn't help it. Her mind went back to last night and his confession about his past. She'd spent the night tossing and turning, going over what he'd said, all he'd endured, and how it had impacted the man he was today. And her heart went out to him, it really did.

But in the end, she kept thinking about one sentence in particular. *What I felt for you, I've never experienced anything like it.* She told herself not to read too much into those words but how could she not?

She was torn between the conflicting facts she knew. He hadn't wanted a real relationship until finding out about the baby. But he said his feelings for her were unique. And he claimed to desire more than co-parenting with her now. Her head spinning, she didn't know what to think or feel.

But when she looked at his handsome face, strong jaw, full lips, eyes that sometimes hid his feelings but too often now seemed to reveal more and more, she couldn't deny she wanted *more* too.

ETHAN WAS DIZZY with anticipation. He held Sienna's hand, his heart beating hard as his gaze settled on the black-and-white screen where he hoped to catch a glimpse of their child.

The doctor palpated Sienna's belly, then said, "It's too early to hear the heartbeat, so we'll have you back in a couple of weeks for a Doppler and another sonogram." Dr. Finley's hand moved the wand around. "You won't see much today, but we'll know he or she is in there. Week three is when fertilization really begins."

A few minutes later, the doctor paused the wand. "There!" She hit a few buttons and captured the image on the screen. "The beginning of your baby."

"Oh my God! Ethan, look. Our baby." Sienna breathed out the words, her cheeks flushed, her face glowing.

As much as she was pushing him away, she wanted his child. That gave him something to work with, he thought, because he had every intention of keeping them both.

The doctor hit a key and a printer sent out two small photographs. "Proof positive," she said, waving the papers in the air before handing them to him.

With her easy grin, Ethan relaxed even more than he had after she'd reassured them about the cancer risk. He hadn't let his mind go *there*, but now that the doctor had negated the chances, he found himself able to breathe.

And with the pictures in his hand, although he couldn't decipher a damned thing on them, reality hit him hard.

He was going to be a father. Sienna was going to be a mother. And he was going to do everything he could not just to bring them together as a couple because of the baby, but to convince her they had a future. Because he wanted a future with this vivacious, gorgeous woman who had brought him back to life.

After wiping down the wand and replacing it in its holder, Dr. Finley stood. "I'll give you some time alone. The nurse will be in soon to draw blood, and I'll give you a call only if there's something to be concerned about, but from what I've seen so far, I'm not worried. Make an appointment for eight weeks and I'll see you then.

Left alone, Ethan did what he'd been wanting to do. He leaned over and pressed his lips against Sienna's, sliding his mouth over hers, licking at the seam, and when she parted her lips, he slid his tongue inside.

The kiss was brief, but as far as he was concerned, it said everything he couldn't express in words after the moment they'd just shared. Somehow, someway, he was going to step up his game and undo the damage he'd done by telling her he didn't want a relationship and asking her to stay in the shadows.

Today was the beginning. Not just of the life they'd created but the one Ethan was determined to have with this woman by his side.

Whether she knew it… or not.

✧   ✧   ✧

ETHAN APPEARED TO be a man on a mission. He was in Sienna's space twenty-four seven, not just working, although plenty of that was accomplished, but he was making himself indispensable to her, bringing her breakfast, taking her to lunch, showing up to drive her to and from work. He was always around. The worst part for Sienna was how much she was coming to enjoy his company and this new, happy Ethan Knight. She even found herself glancing at her clock, anticipating his appearance with lunch in hand.

She'd done just that when her phone rang and she saw her mother's number on the screen. "Hi, Mom," she said as she answered.

"Hi, honey. I know you're at work and I wouldn't ask if it wasn't important, but can you come over? Now?" Her voice hitched and Sienna's heart clenched in her chest.

"Of course. Mom, what's wrong?" But even as Sienna asked, she was rising from her seat and grabbing her purse and keys.

"I'll talk to you when you get here. Drive safe."

She walked quickly out of the office, bumping into Ethan as she rounded the corner to the front doors. "Whoa," he said, grasping her shoulders. "Where's the fire?"

"Family emergency. I have to get to my mother's." She'd known something was wrong for a while now. Part of her hadn't wanted to ask for fear of what she'd learn and another didn't want to pry.

"I'll take you," he said, grasping her arm and turning around to head back out along with her.

She shook her head. "I'm fine. Honestly, I can drive myself."

"But you don't have to."

She sighed. "What's in the bag?" She gestured to the sack in his hand.

"Chicken sandwiches and French fries."

"Then you can drive and I'll eat the food," she muttered, no longer embarrassed to chow down in front of him. She was always hungry and he knew it.

He shook his head and laughed. "Fine. Let's go. You can direct me."

Once they were on their way, Sienna glanced at Ethan, taken aback anew by his easy demeanor and the changes in him. They'd started on his return to Florida after his weekend in New York and had only blossomed the more time they spent together, the doctor's appointment seemingly shattering the rest of his walls. Too bad hers weren't ready to come down yet, though she had to admit it wasn't easy to keep her distance.

"Do you know why your mother wants to see you?" Ethan asked.

She shook her head, digging into the bag with the French fries, chewing and swallowing a few. "God, these are good."

He chuckled. "Well, I can wait in the car while you talk."

She frowned at him. "Don't be silly. You can wait in the house. If she wants privacy, I'll stash you in the kitchen. Bring your food. You can eat lunch."

164

A little while later, he pulled up in front of her mom's house, an imposing colonial she and her dad had purchased only after the big family reveal. Prior to that they'd lived in a more modest, out-of-the-way home.

Ethan followed her up the walkway, his hand on her back. She was aware of his touch, the strong palm against her shirt that felt more like he was branding her bare skin. She rang the bell and her mother answered … not looking like her mom.

Instead of being immaculately dressed in pants and a blouse, her hair done, her eyes alight with laughter and life, she wore a robe, no makeup, and she'd clearly been crying.

"Mom?" Sienna asked, concerned.

"I really should wait in the car." Ethan turned but Sienna caught his hand, realizing she was going to need his support.

"I know this isn't the right time, but Mom, Ethan drove me over, so I'll have him wait in another room while we talk."

Her mom nodded. "Nice to see you again, Ethan. I assume we'll get to know each other well. But right now Sienna's brothers are waiting in the family room."

"I understand," Ethan said in a gruff voice.

"Brothers? Jason's in town?" Sienna asked, realizing how dire things must be if her brother had flown in from New York. She shot Ethan a concerned look.

He squeezed her shoulder and let her lead him to the kitchen, where she left him and joined her siblings in the family room.

"Jase!" She jumped into her brother's arms and he groaned.

"Did you put on weight?"

"Rude!" She shot him a raspberry and wriggled down to her feet. "I know you know I'm pregnant."

He scowled. "Yes, and I'm going to kick the ass of the man who took advantage of you."

Alex nodded beside him. "I've been good but it hasn't been easy."

"You two will do no such thing. He's in the kitchen because he drove me here. And you're going to be nice to him. N.I.C.E.," she said in case they needed it spelled out.

"Boys, listen to your sister."

At the sound of her mother's voice, Sienna was reminded of why they were here. She sat down next to Jason, who reached out and held her hand, which she appreciated given the nerves overtaking her.

"What's going on, Mom?" Sienna couldn't stand to be in the dark any longer. "You're not sick, are you?" Sudden nausea overtook her at the thought.

"No, no, nothing like that, although you're going to be upset." Her mother paced the floor, her silk robe

166

flowing around her. "I know you've noticed things with your father have been… different lately. More strained." She wound her fingers tightly together. "Well, we're getting divorced," she said, her voice catching on the last word.

"What? Why?" Sienna asked, completely caught off guard. Her parents had had a loving marriage. Had they come together in an unconventional and unfortunate way? Yes. But they'd seemed to love each other.

Her mother glanced from Jason to Alex and an uneasy feeling twisted in Sienna's stomach. "What is it? And why are you looking at them like they have the answers?"

Jason squeezed Sienna's hand tighter. "Dad's having an affair," he said, meeting her gaze.

Sienna blinked. "Wait, you know? Did Mom tell you before I got here?"

Alex shook his head. "It's a really long story."

She wrenched her hand free of Jason's. "Well, I have all the time in the world, so talk."

Her mother lowered herself into a chair. "Tyler ran into your father at a restaurant with another woman and it was obvious they weren't just friends or business partners. He told his full siblings."

Sienna narrowed her gaze. All her half siblings knew. Of them all, Avery hurt the most that she'd kept the news from Sienna, because they were the closest.

She swallowed hard. "And then what happened?" She wasn't about to put the pieces together herself.

Jason and Alex exchanged guilty looks.

"Ian told his wife, and she told me," Alex said.

"And Alex told me," Jason added.

"And we agreed I should tell Mom." Alex rubbed his hands together, clearly knowing now withholding the information from her had been a mistake.

But they'd done it and betrayal settled in her bones. "You all kept it from me. All of you." The brothers she'd grown up with. Her best friend. Ian. The rest of her half siblings. "*Why?*" she asked, tears forming in her eyes.

Her mother walked over and sat on her other side, putting an arm around her shoulders. "At first you were away at school and we didn't want you distracted."

She set her jaw. "And then?"

"We didn't want to upset you."

"So you treated me like a baby and not the adult that I am," she said, her voice rising. Maybe she should be focusing on feeling badly for her mother and the divorce, and she did, but right now she hurt.

"What's going on?" Ethan showed up in the doorway, looking pissed. "Why do you sound upset?" His gaze zeroed in on Sienna.

"Who is this?" Jason asked, rising to his feet. He hadn't been at the hospital when she'd been brought in, so he hadn't met Ethan.

Alex stood as well. Both of her brothers, arms folded across their chests, glared at Ethan.

"Jason, this is Ethan Knight. Ethan, my brother Jason. You already met Alex at the hospital," Sienna said, gesturing between them.

Her brother narrowed his gaze. "This is the baby's father?"

Ethan stepped up, extending a hand to Jason.

Her sibling's scowl and deliberately ignoring Ethan's greeting radiated *fuck off* in its anger and animosity, and Sienna groaned. "Jason, come on. Be nice."

"We'll discuss that later. Right now, there's no reason for him to be here. It's family business," Jason said.

"If Sienna is upset, there's every reason for me to be here." Ethan held his own with her siblings, and was it wrong for Sienna to find that just a little arousing?

"Ethan, it's just that…" Her mother's voice trailed off. "We made a mistake and Sienna is understandably upset."

Her words made Ethan's scowl worsen. "She's not supposed to be stressed."

"I'm an adult! I can handle the information that affects my life and the people around me, and I'm sick and tired of being babied! I'm not sick with cancer anymore!" she yelled, then stormed out of the room without looking back.

Her heart pounded rapidly in her chest and her pulse was racing as she headed out to the car. It was obvious to her that her family still considered her a child and incapable of handling important news until there was no choice but to pull her in. And that stung.

Tears spilled out of her eyes, which annoyed her, too. She was too emotional but Ethan was right. She wasn't supposed to get upset.

Waiting for him, she lowered herself to the curb and focused on calming herself down. For the baby's sake. As far as her family was concerned, she was furious and she needed space.

ETHAN STARED AT the three people closest to Sienna in disbelief. "Two of you know firsthand the doctor said no stress." His gaze went from Alex to Sienna's mother. He glanced at Jason. "You don't know but I'm guessing the message was relayed. So what gives?"

Jason, the man Ethan had never seen before, glared at him, but Alex looked contrite.

"Shit," the man muttered. "I have a wife. I know

170

better than to keep secrets."

Jason rolled his eyes. "We agreed she didn't need to be upset."

"Well, maybe you need to agree on the fact that she's a grown woman you need to treat with respect." Ethan glanced at Sienna's mother.

"He's right, boys. We made a calculated error. We meant well, but she should have been told from the beginning that your father is, once again, a no-good, cheating, lying bastard."

Ethan winced. Well, that gave him the information he needed. This mess had something to do with Robert Dare, and from the sound of it, he was back to his old ways.

"Are you three okay? Can I go after Sienna? And you'll call her later and make peace? I don't want her worked up."

The three of them nodded.

It was Alex who stepped up. "I'm not happy that you knocked up my baby sister but you seem to care about her."

"I do. I'm going to protect her and do right by her. And if that means she needs a break from her family, that's what she's going to get," Ethan warned them and he had an idea about how to do just that.

"I'm going to hold you to those words," Jason said. "I may be in New York but my reach is long."

Ethan didn't take offense to the warning, but he wasn't about to inform Jason that his home base was New York as well. That was news for another time.

Instead he turned to Sienna's mother. "I'm sorry for what you're going through, and when Sienna calms down, she'll realize she's upset about that, too. I'm sure you'll hear from her or you can reach out. Right now I'm going to check on her," Ethan said, and strode out to the car, where he found Sienna sitting on the curb, her eyes damp with tears.

"Hey." He lowered himself beside her, his ass half on the grass, half on the curb. Placing a hand on the back of her neck, he asked, "Are you okay?"

She sniffed. "Yeah. I'm angry at my family. They had information they kept from me for no good reason I can think of. All of them, the other side, too."

"About your dad."

She nodded. "And my parents are getting divorced."

"I'm sorry about that."

"My dad is an asshole. And frankly my mother got him when he was cheating and you know what they say. Once a cheater, always a cheater." She hung her head. "I'm upset for my mom, but right now I'm more hurt than anything else."

"Sounds to me like you need to get away from the stress." He glanced at her in time to catch a slight

172

smile.

"That would be nice."

"Ever been to Colorado?" he asked.

She shook her head.

"What do you say we go visit my brother? His father-in-law runs a bed-and-breakfast there. Parker and his wife, Emily, bought land nearby and built a house. I think I mentioned to you, she's pregnant, too. I think it would do us good to get out of here for a little while."

She glanced up at him, eyes wide. "What about work?"

He shrugged, knowing that wasn't an issue. "I think once I talk to Ian, he'll agree you need a break."

She leaned her head against his arm and he pulled her tight into his side. "Family's hard. Life is hard."

He nodded. "Can't disagree. All we can do is make the best of the hand we're dealt and move forward from there." And he wanted to move forward with Sienna.

The only way to change her mind-set about him and what he wanted was to take her away from here and her family drama, introduce her to his brother and his wife, and romance her out west.

Chapter Nine

SIENNA BOUNCED IN the seat of the rental, excited to be in Colorado and away from her family. She hadn't ghosted them. Instead she'd called her mom, talked about the divorce, and accepted her mother's apology for keeping Sienna in the dark. Her brothers and half siblings, she wasn't so gracious with. They'd left her out and hurt her feelings and she wasn't ready to be generous in her forgiveness. She'd leave them hanging until she returned home. By then she could let everything go, assuming they promised to treat her like the adult she was.

Avery had groveled already, feeling guilty and admitting she'd caved to Ian's demands. Knowing how difficult her oldest half sibling could be, Sienna had accepted her best friend/half sister's apology. Which didn't mean she was over it. Just that she'd let Avery off the hook.

But now Sienna had taken a private jet to Colorado and a rental SUV to Montlake, where the Ruby Rose Inn was located. They approached the wood-framed structure painted a deep red with white trim, blooming bushes, and fresh green grass. The closer she came, the more she realized everything was painted new, renovated, and gorgeous.

"It's beautiful!" Sienna said, gushing because she really did love the rustic look.

"When Parker got here, the place was falling apart. Emily and her dad were struggling and Parker immediately stepped up and helped infuse the place with much-needed money. This is the result," Ethan said with pride in his voice.

He pulled the SUV into a parking spot, put it in park, and turned it off. "You should know, I'm not so sure Emily likes me," he said, resting a hand on the steering wheel and meeting Sienna's gaze.

"What? Why?" She blinked in surprise. He'd been so eager to come here, she hadn't expected to hear that.

A dark flush stained his cheeks. "I might have put my foot in my mouth the day I arrived. Add to that the mood I was in during their wedding? Yeah. She probably hates me."

Sienna heard the pain in his voice and reached out to clasp his hand. "If Parker is anything like you, I'm sure he's explained things and smoothed the situation over. She's probably already forgiven you and you don't even know it."

He rolled his shoulders, obviously tense. "I was really an ass," he muttered.

She burst out laughing. "Somehow that doesn't shock me. Come on. Let's go in. Whatever smoothing Parker hasn't done, I'll handle. How's that?"

He eased over and pressed his lips to hers, taking her by surprise. Unable to resist, she leaned close and opened her lips for him. He slid his tongue against hers and groaned into her mouth. Too soon, he straightened, breaking the kiss.

"What was that for?" she asked, breathless.

"Because I really don't deserve you but I'm glad you're here with me anyway."

Before she could reply, he turned and opened the door, hopping out. She joined him, meeting him by the trunk, where he pulled their luggage from the back. She inhaled the fresh air and sighed, already falling in love with the open spaces and beautiful scenery.

Once again she'd surprised Ethan with her minimalist packing, and he wheeled their two carry-ons toward the front door of the inn.

As if on cue, the door opened and a middle-aged man greeted them. "Welcome!" he said, joining them on the porch. "Ethan, how are you?" the man asked.

"Good. And you?"

"Great. And who is this beautiful lady?" the man asked.

"James Stevens, meet Sienna Dare. James is Emily's father," Ethan explained.

James shook her hand. "You're going to love it here. Emily already stopped by with Snickerdoodles for the two of you and said she and Parker would come once they knew you'd arrived."

"I'll text him," Ethan said of his brother, pulling out his phone.

James then showed them to a grouping of rooms on one side of the inn. "We don't have guests until this weekend, so pick any rooms you want."

Ethan thanked James and said he could handle it, and James took off, leaving them in the hallway.

"I'd like it if we could share a room," Ethan immediately said when they were alone. "No pressure or anything but I want to be with you. However I can get you."

She swallowed hard. Prior to this trip, she hadn't given the rooming situation any thought. Did she want to insist on her own room, knowing Ethan was sleeping next door or across the hall?

No, no she did not.

He was making such an effort to be the perfect guy for her, and though she knew he'd be returning to New York, why couldn't she take advantage of the time they had together? Her heart was his, whether he wanted it for keeps or not. She wouldn't push him, knew that wasn't smart with a man as wounded and hurt as Ethan had been.

Sometimes spontaneous judgment calls were the best ones, she mused, having come to a decision. "Umm, I was thinking. You know that proposition you made me? An affair while you're here?"

He blinked in surprise. "Yes?" he asked hesitantly. He clearly had no idea where she was going with this line of thought.

"Well, I'd like to take you up on the offer. Be with you while we're here and when we get back to Miami. Once you have to go back to New York, no pressure or strings," she said, forcing the painful words from her mouth.

He'd told her he hadn't been ready for a relationship after his wife died, and though he was tied to Sienna due to the baby, she'd never, ever want to trap him in any way.

But that didn't mean she couldn't give in to what her body ... and her heart desired now.

✧   ✧   ✧

ETHAN DIDN'T LIKE his own words thrown back at him. *I'd like to take you up on the offer. Be with you while we're here and when we get home. Once you have to go back to New York, no pressure or strings.* Jesus, it sucked.

And he deserved every painful word.

He studied her for so long she grew uncomfortable, shifting from foot to foot. Until a blush stained her cheeks. Until he could decide how to handle this. Because he wanted more than just a fuck while they were together.

What he didn't know or understand was how much more. He needed time.

So he did the only thing he could do.

He stepped closer. Her light fragrance surrounded him, and at his nearness, her breath caught in her throat. Her lips parted. And he sealed his mouth over hers.

He drank from her, tipping her head to the side, thrusting his tongue in, and taking all that she offered and giving in return. He backed her up to the wall and aligned his body against hers. His chest to her chest. His cock to her sex. His lips never leaving hers, tackling her tongue and devouring her.

"Hey, E! You up there?" Parker yelled from downstairs.

Ethan ignored him. He slid a hand to her waist and pulled her shirt up, his rougher hands gliding along her skin.

"Ethan!"

Sienna ducked beneath his arm and drew in a deep breath. "Is that your brother?" she asked through puffy lips and desire-laden eyes.

"Yeah, cockblocker," Ethan muttered.

She rolled her eyes. "I'm going to pull myself together before I meet them. Go distract them or something." Grabbing her suitcase, she rolled it into the nearest room.

The one he knew had a king-size bed.

With that thought on his mind, he adjusted his dick and headed downstairs to see his brother.

"Ethan!" Emily met up with him as he hit the bottom step.

Contrary to what he'd told Sienna, she greeted him like they were old friends, pulling him into a sisterly hug. "I'm so glad you came to visit."

He stepped back and studied his brother's wife. She was the antithesis of the New York woman, no makeup, jeans and a flowing top disguising the beginnings of her pregnancy, her hair pulled up on top of her head in a messy but cute bun. She was adorable and fit Parker to a T. Much more than Ethan had thought when he'd first laid eyes on her and assumed she was after his brother for his money. He winced at the awful memory of Emily overhearing him say exactly that.

"Hi, Emily. It's good to see you, too." He stepped back, catching sight of his brother on the other side of the room. "Hey … umm … about my general shitty attitude every time we've been together until now. I'm sorry," Ethan said.

Her eyes opened wide. "I think that's the nicest thing anyone's said to me." She grinned at him and shook her head. "No apologies necessary. No rehashing allowed, either."

She was a generous soul and Ethan was glad his brother had found her. "Thanks," he said.

"Aww, you can be sweet." Sienna's voice sounded from behind him and he realized she'd overheard him.

Oh, well. It wasn't like he hadn't shown her what an asshole he could be firsthand. Now she saw his better side.

He gestured for her to join him, and when she did, he pulled her hand into his. "Sienna Dare, this is my sister-in-law Emily, and the quiet guy over there is my middle brother, Parker."

Parker waved a hand in the air and strode over, as Sienna and Emily said their hellos.

"So you're the woman who got this guy's head back on straight. I'm happy to meet you," Parker said, a mouthful for the sibling they called Switzerland because he rarely took sides and sat on the proverbial fence. Of course, there was also the fact that he'd been an Olympic champion skier before he'd blown out his knee, twice, that contributed to the nickname.

"Hi," Sienna said.

"Welcome to Colorado. Can't wait to show you

guys around," Parker said. "Although you've already seen the best part now that you've checked out the Ruby Rose Inn."

Emily laughed. "Wait until they taste my cookies. Then they'll really fall in love."

Sienna grinned. "Cookies? I'd love some cookies."

One thing about his girl, Ethan thought, she could eat. Especially now that she was pregnant. Although she wasn't showing at all yet, because Sebastian knew Ethan had gotten Sienna pregnant, and he'd told Sierra when he went home last weekend, Ethan had already told Parker as well.

To his brother's credit, he didn't say a word about it. Instead he and Emily were making Sienna feel at home.

"Come on," Emily said, hooking her arm into Sienna's. "Let's go eat." She patted her small belly. "This one keeps me hungry."

Sienna merely blushed, shot Ethan a glance, and headed for the kitchen with Emily.

Parker turned to Ethan. "Want a scotch?"

He shook his head. "I'm good. Get one if you want."

"Nah, I'm fine, too. Just trying to be a good host. Not that it's my place but it is my second home." He led Ethan to the big room by the windows facing the front lawn and the fireplace in the corner and they took seats facing each other.

"So what brings you to my neck of the woods? Not that I'm complaining," Parker said.

Ethan glanced over, and though the space was open-concept, it was huge, and Sienna was busy at the kitchen table, talking to Emily in hushed murmurs. He could talk to his brother without being overheard.

"A couple of reasons, to be honest. Sienna needed a break from some family drama, for one thing. I needed to get her alone and receptive to seeing I'm a decent guy, for another."

Parker narrowed his gaze. "What did you do?" he asked, sounding resigned.

"Sebastian didn't tell you?"

Parker shrugged. "Maybe I wanted to hear your version, too."

"Won't get any better in the second telling," Ethan muttered.

Parker shook his head. "Look, I know you were dealt a shit hand but it's time to get over it."

"And I have. Mostly." Ethan couldn't quite wrap his head around the idea of having a wife and kid, but he didn't have to make that leap yet. "I'm working on it."

Parker slapped his knee. "Well, whatever the reason, I'm happy to have you here. I took a couple of days off so we can show you around and have some fun. Sound good?"

Ethan nodded. Sounded good.

Having Sienna to himself sounded even better.

✦   ✦   ✦

COLORADO PROVIDED A soothing balm to Sienna's heart and soul. The fresh air, the green grass, the lack of humidity common to her home state, all made for a refreshing change. One she hadn't realized she needed. She loved Ethan's brother Parker and his wife, Emily, as much as she'd liked Sierra. She hadn't had a chance to get to know Sebastian, but she assumed he was as amiable as the rest of the Knight clan. She could see what a shock Ethan's behavior this past year must have been to the family. Parker was thrilled, in his words, to have his brother back. He'd even called it a new and improved version.

Sienna liked all parts of Ethan, even the dark, surly man she'd first met. She wouldn't have slept with him otherwise. There was something about him that she'd been drawn to from the beginning, and now that he was smiling and enjoying life, she felt like she had the best of him.

They ate dinner at Parker and Emily's favorite restaurant and made plans to drive around tomorrow, see Parker's new ski shop and Emily and her best friend Harper's Bake and Brew. But today had been a long travel day, and after dinner, Sienna was exhausted, something Ethan seemed to pick up on.

"Do you want us to come back to the inn?" Parker asked as they walked out of the restaurant.

Ethan shook his head. "I think Sienna needs sleep." He wrapped an arm around her waist, pulling her against him.

It was all she could do not to lay her head on his shoulder and fall asleep right here.

They said their good nights, Parker and Emily promising to come over around ten tomorrow morning. Good, Sienna thought. She could sleep in.

They walked into the inn, James having left the door unlocked for them. He told them he turned in early and instructed them to lock up when they got home. No sooner had Ethan turned the dead bolt than he picked up Sienna in his arms and began carrying her up the stairs.

"What are you doing?" she asked.

"Putting you to bed. You're dead on your feet," he said in a gruff voice. "I appreciate you pushing through dinner with my brother, but I can see you're exhausted."

She wrapped her arms around his neck, holding on as he walked them up the stairs and into their shared bedroom. He laid her down on the bed.

She rolled over and closed her eyes for a minute

and the next thing she knew, she woke up to a pitch-black room. She'd obviously fallen fast asleep. As she inventoried herself and her surroundings, she realized that Ethan had undressed her, leaving her in her underwear alone. She wasn't even wearing her bra.

Beside her, under the covers, Ethan slept, facing the other direction. A quick check and she realized he wore boxer briefs and nothing more.

She bit down on her lower lip, now completely awake. What were her options? She could attempt to fall back to sleep ... or she could wake him up and indulge. She had to admit she was horny, a state she hadn't let herself think about since there was nothing to be done about it ... nothing but her trusty vibrator, anyway. But now?

She hesitated for just a second before deciding. Indulging it was. She slid closer to where he slept, his body moving in even cadence with his breathing, and placed her lips against his warm back. When he didn't move, she slid her lips over his skin, alternately licking and kissing his flesh.

Without warning, he groaned, and suddenly he flipped over, trapping her between his big body and the mattress. "Do you want something?" he asked in a sleep-roughened voice.

"You."

"Somehow, someway ... you've got me," he said,

and since she didn't know if he was still half-asleep, she didn't let herself read too much into his words. And then he began to glide down her body, tasting her as he went, and she stopped thinking at all.

He kissed and nibbled his way from her mouth, down her neck, to her collarbone, where he bit down lightly, causing her to squirm, before moving on. He licked down her chest, pausing at her breasts.

He slid a tongue over her nipple and she moaned. He bit down lightly and her hips jerked upward, her sex coming into direct contact with his hard erection.

"I'm so much more sensitive now," she whispered in awe.

"Yeah? Let's see." He continued his assault until she couldn't stand the intensity and she grasped his head and pulled him away.

Chuckling deep in his throat, he merely switched to the other side and gave it the same sensual treatment. Her body felt electrified. The tiny pulses of need she experienced in her breasts had an equal pulsing of desire in her sex. She writhed beneath him, grinding herself up against him, trying to gain the friction she needed in order to come.

"Bad girl," he said gruffly and slipped his hand into her panties. "So hot, so wet." He slid his fingers back and forth, gathering the moisture and rubbing it over her clit.

She sucked in a startled breath as the rising sensation began to take over.

"Don't stop," she whispered, rocking her hips in time to the circling of his finger. All she could concentrate on was the perfection of the pad of his finger bringing her higher and higher.

"Never," he said, his voice a dark promise. "Not until you come." He slicked his finger back and forth over the tight bud, moving faster and faster until she exploded, her body a mass of perfect sensation, taking her higher and higher.

Keeping his promise, he rubbed her clit until she couldn't handle the feeling anymore and she collapsed against the bed, pulling her body away from the sensation.

He rose up and yanked off his underwear, coming back over her, his cock poised at her entrance. No sooner had he begun to enter her than her sensitized body reacted and she began that impossible climb once more.

"No," she whispered. "No way can I come again."

"Yes." He thrust deep, filling her completely. Without waiting, he picked up a steady rhythm, his cock hitting the right spot inside her that had her seeing stars.

"Yes," she agreed, gripping his back with her fingernails. "God, yes."

He rocked his body into her and she'd never felt anything better. It was like she was made for him. Everything he did took her higher and closer to climax. He braced his hands on either side of her and picked up his tempo, thrusting faster, harder, deeper.

"Ethan!" She screamed his name as her body let go for a second time, taking her over, lost in him.

Lost in them.

"Jesus," he said, gritting his teeth, as if waiting for her to finish before letting go.

And then he did and he slammed into her over and over, owning her completely.

He collapsed, catching himself before he fell on top of her, and rolled to the side, pulling her into him.

His warm breath fanned her neck, and she'd never felt so needed as he held her in his arms. But she warned herself not to get used to it. As much as she wanted this forever, it wasn't in the cards.

ETHAN COULD SEE why his brother loved the mountains. For a brief stretch of time, he could breathe. Holding on to Sienna's hand, they toured Parker's ski shop, the scale of which impressed him because he knew his brother had expanded since going into business just a few short months ago with a new partner. It was as if Parker had just been existing until

Ethan had sent him to Colorado to find a resort for a company retreat. He'd had car trouble, ended up at Emily's dad's resort, and rediscovered life.

Sort of like finding Sienna had caused Ethan to find himself again. He glanced at the woman by his side as they pulled up to Harper and Em's Bake and Brew, Emily's new business in town. Sienna watched the scenery pass with interested eyes, her dark hair falling around her face. Although he'd been to town before, he found himself viewing it through her fresh eyes.

"Emily mentioned this place is new?" Sienna asked, her eyes wide as they took in the huge signage over the shop.

"Harper had a small coffee shop. Emily baked at home and brought her goods here daily for Harper to sell. Their dream was to take over the space next door that was available but Emily couldn't afford it. Parker insisted she let him help. They're still arguing over whether or not it's a loan." Ethan shook his head and laughed. "I'm sure I know who'll win that one."

"For a quiet guy, I take it Parker can be pretty insistent?"

Ethan nodded. "Especially when it comes to Emily and keeping her happy. He'll do anything."

Her expression softened as he spoke, and he could see in her eyes how much she wanted that for herself.

Before he could think it through, a knock sounded on the window.

"Hey, you two coming in?" Parker asked through the glass.

Ethan refrained from shooting his brother the finger for interrupting. Instead he glanced at Sienna. "Are you ready?"

She nodded, then grinned. "I'm starving."

He rolled his eyes and they climbed out of the SUV.

SIENNA TOOK IN the restaurant with greedy eyes. It was homey, with wood chairs and tables, yet modern, including phone-charging stations and USB ports, and very neighborhood friendly, selling local artisan cups and portraits on the walls. She loved the intimate space on sight, and she envied Emily that she had something all her own.

Though she hadn't wanted to admit it to herself, Sienna wasn't as fulfilled by working for Ian as she wanted to be. She'd been thrilled by his excitement over her ideas, but the execution wasn't all that satisfying. Getting out of town and having time to herself to think had only brought that truth to the forefront of her mind. Though she was grateful to Ian for the opportunity and she loved contributing to his new stadium, she didn't want to work in online marketing and merchandising after this project ended.

Before she could overthink things, a pretty blonde met them as they entered, greeting Parker with a hug and reintroducing herself to Ethan, who she'd apparently met at Parker and Emily's wedding.

Then she turned to Sienna, welcoming her with a warm smile. "I'm so excited you all came by! I'm Harper, Emily's partner and best friend."

"So nice to meet you. I love your café."

Harper beamed. "Thank you. I'm pretty proud of it myself. Emily and I worked hard getting it ready for opening."

"I bet it's amazing, working with your best friend." Sienna and Avery had gotten together to do charity work for the hospital where Sienna had had her stem cell transplant, organizing a prom-like party for sick children who couldn't leave the hospital to attend their own proms. Avery's now-husband, Grey, head of a huge rock band, had performed, and there'd been nothing more satisfying than seeing the hopeful, happy look on the kids' faces. They'd gone so far as to find businesses to donate dresses, brought in makeup artists to help them feel beautiful, and the night had been a huge success.

She sighed at the memory.

"Sienna?" Ethan's voice brought her back to the

present.

"Yes?"

"We're going to a table. Are you okay?" he asked, sounding worried, his intense gaze focused on hers.

She smiled. "Yeah. When I thought about Emily working with her best friend, I remembered the time Avery and I put together a charity event. It was amazingly fulfilling." She shook her head. "Sorry. I got distracted."

He gave her a concerned look, then led her to the table, where Emily joined them, apron on and a dusting of flour on her cheek. Parker pulled her onto his lap.

After another woman served them, they sat around together, talking and laughing, and Sienna almost felt like she and Ethan belonged together ... except despite his arm around her shoulder and the sweet way he'd lean into her and include her in conversation, she forced herself to remember they weren't a permanent couple like Parker and Emily. She and Ethan were temporary.

Despite the upset that thought caused, Sienna devoured the most delicious banana muffin and took another one for the road when it was time to leave, causing Ethan to chuckle. He found her eating habits more amusing than he should.

She stuffed the bag with the muffin in her purse

and climbed into the car. Ethan shut the door behind her.

Once he was settled in, he faced her before turning on the ignition. "What was that about in there? The charity project. You never mentioned it before but that look on your face? You were glowing."

She smiled. "I was remembering a project I did with my best friend, Avery. We put on a prom for kids who were undergoing chemo and treatment and couldn't go to their own proms. It was amazing. That we could take them away from their pain and problems for one night? It was so sweet."

He reached out and grasped her hand. "I like that part of you, giving back because you know what it's like to be in their position."

She swallowed hard, sobering, as she said, "You have no idea how lonely it can be. I had my mom. Avery had her mom when she donated. But so many children, their parents work. They can't be there for them day and night while they're in the hospital and some are there for months." She sniffed, her eyes watering. "You're in pain and alone. It's awful. So if I could bring them even a minute's happiness? It's worth it."

He tipped his head to the side. "Can I ask you something?"

"Sure."

"Why did you major in business? Why not in something where you could eventually put your focus into the charity work you love?" He studied her, his gaze warm, as he obviously understood what was in her heart.

"Because my father was a businessman. My grades were stellar. I did what everyone expected me to do." She shrugged. "You know college, you have to pick a major, and sometimes it's easier to do what makes sense. You're not always old enough to know what it is you really want." She shook her head. "I didn't even realize how I was feeling until I was away from it all and came here. And the charity thing didn't hit me until I saw Harper and Emily working together."

He nodded. "I get it. I can't deny what you suggested for Ian's stadium is brilliant, but there's a lot to be said for being happy in life, too."

She managed a smile. "I'll definitely see the stadium project through. What happens after that? We'll see."

Just like she'd see what happened after Ethan's part in the project was over and he went back to New York. Her heart twisted at the thought.

"Ready to get back to the inn?" he asked.

They were going home first thing in the morning, and she planned to enjoy the time they had left because it was starting to feel like the clock for Sienna and Ethan was ticking down.

Chapter Ten

S IENNA ARRIVED HOME, knowing she had to deal with her family issues. She called her brothers, Alex and Jason, and read them the riot act about hiding things from her, keeping her in the dark, and treating her like a baby. And while she was at it, she informed them both she expected them to be nice to Ethan. As the father of her baby, they had to accept him. No choice.

Considering how upset she'd been when she left and how protective they'd seen Ethan be over her well-being, both brothers gave in to her demands. They also apologized and admitted they were wrong. She took the win. It wasn't often her siblings groveled.

The rest of the family? Well, Olivia apologized at work. Ian grumbled his *I might have been a bit over protective*, and everyone else admitted they were wrong. They'd taken their cues from Ian and were sorry.

With that behind her, she turned her focus to finishing up the stadium project, and on Saturday, she'd called Avery to discuss picking up their charity work again. Avery suggested they go over to the Meridian Hotel, owned by Robert Dare, to talk. Since her father had been scarce, Sienna wasn't worried about running into him.

But luck wasn't on her side. She had just pulled up in her car and climbed out when she caught sight of her father.

"Sienna!" He called her name and walked over. Wearing his usual suit and tie, his salt-and-pepper hair styled perfectly, he looked like the man who'd raised her. Unfortunately she'd come to discover the father she adored was a duplicitous human being.

"Hi."

He grasped her shoulders and looked her over. "I heard the news."

"And yet I haven't heard from you."

He glanced everywhere but at her. "I've been busy."

She narrowed her gaze. "That seems to be a pattern for you. Get busy with one family, forget about the one you left behind. I understand you've moved on again. Best of luck." She turned and walked away, leaving him stunned and speechless behind her.

Her heart beat rapidly in her chest as she headed inside, hearing him call her name, but she ignored it, realizing for the first time how her half siblings really must have felt over the years. Betrayed, hurt, devastated... It was a wonder they'd all managed to forge relationships with each other at all. Certainly, it was no thanks to their father.

She rushed into the hotel, wishing she and her sister had decided to meet anywhere else, and caught sight of Avery at a table outside on the patio.

She walked through the restaurant and joined her half sister, who looked up from her phone. "Oh, hi!"

"Hi." She slid into a chair and let out a breath. "I just ran into Dad." She wrinkled her nose. "I can't cope. And now that I experienced everything you once did firsthand, I feel even worse."

Avery smiled sadly. "Listen, he's our father. That doesn't mean we have to have anything to do with him, but I think it's a decision each of us needs to make on our own."

"Well, I pretty much just told him to have a nice life."

"If you weren't pregnant, I'd say let's drink to that," Avery muttered. "Instead, let's change the subject. What did you want to talk about?"

"Charity. Doing another cancer-related event like we did around prom time."

Avery's eyes lit up at the idea. "Did you have anything specific in mind?"

"Well, yes. But it needs work. It started as a thought." She glanced down and rubbed her belly, which wasn't yet visible through her clothes, but she'd already lost her waist.

"Tell me more."

"What about moms of kids with cancer? Who steps up for them? Who makes sure they have what they need, be it a day off from work to be with their child or a spa day where they can just relax for an hour or two and take a break from the daily hurt and pain?" She waved her hands, gesturing excitedly as she spoke. "So what if we get local vendors – massage therapists and hair salons – to sponsor something called Ma Spa Day to treat the moms in need, and hit up the big corporations to donate money to pay for women's time off and their relaxation time?"

"I love it! I'm in," Avery immediately said.

"Great. Can we meet again and hash out details? I need to go talk to my mother," Sienna said, her confrontation with her father still on her mind.

She might not want a relationship with Robert Dare, but she did love her mom despite her faults. Her plan was to make sure everything with her mom was good, explain that she wasn't all that surprised her dad had cheated – after all, that was what he'd done to his first wife – and help her mother move on.

"Sure. Just call me and we'll get to work," Avery said with a smile. "I'm meeting Grey here for drinks, so I'll just hang out."

Sienna smiled. "Give your husband a hug for me."

"Speaking of hunky guys," Avery said.

Sienna rolled her eyes. "I didn't know we were."

"You said Grey. That's a hunk to me. Anyway, how's your man?" Avery leaned onto the table, clearly dying for information on Sienna and Ethan.

She placed her bag down and sighed. "I wish I knew. Ever since we returned from Colorado, he's been just as attentive and wonderful as he was before. I'm falling head over heels and I don't know what I'm going to do when he goes back to New York, let alone raise a baby with the man when I want so much more."

Avery took a sip of water from the glass that was on the table in front of her. "Are you sure he doesn't want what you want?"

"I can't ask him. I told him I don't have those expectations. If he wants a future, he's going to have to come to me."

ETHAN PICKED UP Sienna's favorite choices in Chinese food and arrived at her apartment. She'd given him a key, so he let himself inside and set up the food on the counter. She walked in after him, looking tired, as she tossed her keys on the counter and her handbag on the sofa.

"Long day."

"I have food," he said, as if that would solve everything. Sometimes in her pregnant state, it did.

They settled into neighboring chairs. He'd even set the table, something he never did before, and waited for her to pick her food.

She loaded her plate, mumbling about family issues and he figured she'd talk to him when she was ready.

He bit into a spare rib and she said, "I ran into my father today."

"Seriously?" He put down the rib and wiped his face on a napkin. "What happened?"

"He treated me the way I've seen him treat the other side of the family all these years. Said he heard I was pregnant, I said funny, I haven't heard from you, but then that's your MO. You find someone new and forget the family you have." She shrugged as if it didn't matter, but he could see it really did. "Then I told him best of luck and walked away."

"That had to have hurt," he murmured.

"Karma maybe. Not to me, but now I know what my half siblings really felt like all these years and it sucks." She looked up at him with damp eyes. "For us he was a good dad. Until he wasn't." She drew a deep breath. "Then I went to Mom's. And though I told her she should have expected as much from my dad, I mean, cheaters cheat ... I also said I'd be there for her while she puts her life back together."

"I'm so sorry, sweetheart." He reached out and pulled her into his lap, wrapping his arms around her. "You have a big family that loves you. I know you'll all figure it out."

But suddenly he sensed that wasn't what she wanted or needed. She needed someone in her life who would put her first. Who'd never hide things from her or treat her like a child.

She needed him.

After the Colorado trip, Ethan had settled into himself. He'd seen what kind of life his brother had built and realized that he wanted the same thing. He thought he'd tried to create that life with Mandy but they were too different. They were both so work focused, their personal lives fell by the wayside. And then Mandy just fell apart and he'd been either unaware or powerless to stop it.

And he realized he could have those things with Sienna. The only thing holding him back now was how much she valued her family. She seemed to need them around her as much as she needed the air she breathed and his life, his business, his family were in New York. Unlike Parker, he couldn't pick up and move. KTT was a New York based corporation.

"I worked out a new charity function with Avery," she said, leaning her head against his shoulder. "It's going to be amazing. We're going to help women whose kids have cancer. I'll explain more later but I know it's going to be awesome."

He groaned, her words merely confirming what he'd already thought. She was so firmly entrenched here, asking her to leave would be difficult if not impossible, but he didn't want to lose her. Somehow he was going to have to figure something out.

He pressed his lips to her hair and breathed in her scent, his cock hardening the longer she sat on his lap. But he wanted her to eat, both for herself and for the baby, otherwise she'd get light-headed and dizzy. He never wanted a repeat of her passing out in his arms.

"Come on," he said, placing her back in her seat. "Eat."

She grinned at him probably because she knew exactly what he was doing and why. Without arguing, she dug in to her food, making him feel better knowing she had her evening meal.

"Have you thought about whether it's a boy or a girl?" she asked, taking him off guard.

He shook his head. "No."

In the beginning, he'd barely let himself acknowledge the idea of a child at all. Now? "A healthy, happy baby will do just fine."

Her smile took his breath away.

"Well, we're in agreement there. Does that mean

we can be surprised?" she asked, sounding hopeful.

"You got it." His heartbeat increased at the idea of an actual child. His child. Their baby.

Suddenly, he couldn't wait.

✧   ✧   ✧

ETHAN SAT IN his office, noting how the summer seemed to fly. He'd spent every free minute when he wasn't working with Sienna getting to know everything about her, watching her grow bigger with his baby… and falling further in love.

He'd gone home to New York a couple of times to handle business issues there, and while gone, he'd missed her like crazy. Something had to give because they were starting to wrap up his company's part in the security of the stadium.

As if on cue, his phone rang and he answered, knowing it was Sebastian. "Hey," Ethan said.

"Hi."

"How's everything at home?" he asked. "Ashley and Sierra okay?"

"All good. No worries. Listen, I just spoke to our supervisor on your pet project. He says things are progressing faster than anticipated. I think everyone was on edge from the California mess and built in extra time, just in case."

"Probably," Ethan muttered. For the first time, the

mention, even indirectly, of Mandy's betrayal didn't gut him the way it used to. It had happened, and miracle of miracles, he'd gotten over it. As for the stadium, he knew just how quickly things were moving, and his stomach cramped at the thought of leaving Miami. Or more to the point, leaving Sienna.

"I was thinking of taking a flight down and checking things out," Sebastian said, unaware of Ethan's conflicted feelings.

His brother's words took him by surprise. "Sure. Come see things for yourself. You'll be happy with the results."

"Good. Does the day after tomorrow work? Ashley's busy with a private client and things are quiet at the office."

"Works for me. I'll pick you up at the airport," he told his brother. "Text me your landing information."

He disconnected the call, staring at the phone, wondering why he was so upset and knowing the answer he just didn't want to face. His time in Miami was coming to an end and he was no closer to a solution with Sienna. If anything, she was even more entrenched in where she lived.

She and Avery had put together an upcoming Labor Day charity event and Ethan couldn't be prouder. She'd hit up corporations and convinced them to donate money that would go to women whose children had cancer, allowing them to take time off from work to spend with their sick kids; she'd gotten local spas and salons to close to the public for one day and donate hours to make women who were normally dragging from exhaustion and had stopped thinking about themselves feel good.

Ma Spa Day, as they called it, had been written up on local blogs, and in print and online newspapers and magazines. Sienna had been offered jobs by a number of nonprofit organizations, and though she hadn't accepted any, she had options.

In Miami.

With a groan, he rose from his seat and was on his way out to pick up lunch when Ian appeared in his office. "Jesus," he said to the other man. "You're like a stealth fighter. I didn't even hear you come in."

Ian chuckled. "Got a minute?" Presuming Ethan did, Ian walked in and settled into a chair.

"Make yourself at home," Ethan muttered and sat down on the edge of his desk. "What can I do for you?"

"You love my sister?" Ian asked.

Leave it to Ian to get right to the point.

Ethan gripped the edge of the desk and faced the man who was so much like Ethan himself when it came to family, it was downright scary. It made it hard for Ethan to get pissed or tell Ian to mind his own fucking business.

"I do love her."

Ian narrowed his gaze. "I expected to have to drag it out of you. Does she know?"

"No."

Ian raised his eyebrows. "Why the hell not?"

Ethan's hands curled harder around the edge of the desk. "You know how badly I want to hit you right now? Or to ask you to get the fuck out of my office?"

Ian grinned. "But you won't. Because you know you'd be doing the exact same thing if the situation were reversed and your sister were involved."

Unable to argue, Ethan just answered the original question. "Why haven't I told her? Because I haven't figured out the future, that's why. What good does it do to bare my soul if I'm leaving? And her entire life is here?"

Ian hung his head and gave it a good shake. "Jesus Christ, now I know why my wife thinks men are dumb shits. Do you have any idea what Sienna would do if you told her you loved her and asked her to marry you? I'll tell you what," the man said before Ethan could jump in. "She'd burst into tears, say yes, pack her bags, and be ready to move to New York in a heartbeat."

Ethan narrowed his gaze, shocked at Ian's words. He'd played out that very scenario in his mind many times lately, and it had never ended that way. "I didn't want to make her choose between me and her family."

"Dumb shit," Ian repeated. "Ask her and see. I'm always right. Besides, I expect you to make an honest woman out of her before she gives birth."

As much as he hated to give Ian credit for anything, Ethan hoped with everything in him that the other man was right.

At the prospect of making Sienna his, anticipation and excitement filled Ethan's veins, and he rose to his feet. "I take it I have your blessing," he said wryly.

Sienna didn't have a father who would step up and do what was best for her. As much as she loved her full brothers, Alex and Jason, Ethan sensed Ian had made himself her parent figure. Ethan needed the man's okay to make Sienna happy. Thank God he had it.

"Not only that, I have the name of a jeweler you can call for a ring. It'll save you a trip to Manhattan." Ian was already searching through his cell phone for the information.

"You really do think of everything." Ethan laughed because at this point he felt like he was looking at his mirror image.

"Take care of my sister, Knight," Ian said as he hit send and forwarded the jeweler's information.

"I'll make it my life's mission," Ethan swore as his

cell phone dinged with the message.

Ian stood. "Gotta go. I have a very pregnant wife at home. Due any day."

Ethan winced at that. "Good luck." He strode over to Ian and shook his hand. "And thank you."

"My pleasure." Ian turned and walked out the door, leaving Ethan with a very important phone number in his hands.

ETHAN PICKED UP Sebastian from the airport and brought him back to Sienna's apartment, where they planned to have dinner. She had a meeting with her sister right after work, and though he was concerned about how many hours she was putting in, she seemed to be able to handle it.

They'd stopped on the way so Sebastian could take a tour of the stadium, and as Ethan had predicted, his brother was pleased. KTT had gotten through the Mandy debacle and come out stronger on the other end.

Ethan poured both himself and Sebastian a scotch and handed his brother the tumbler, then picked up his own. He shoved his hand into his pocket, feeling for the ring he'd picked out this morning before driving to the airport.

He'd yet to tell Sebastian his plan but he intended

to.

Sebastian lifted his glass.

"To you," Sebastian said, taking Ethan off guard. "The irony of this situation isn't lost on me. Right before we landed in Miami, you told me you didn't want kids, yet here you are, making the best of a shit situation. I have to admit, I don't know if I could have done the same if I'd knocked up one of my one-night stands."

A loud gasp sounded from the doorway. Both men turned to find Sienna, wearing a long nightshirt, staring in horror at Ethan and his brother.

"Sienna. I didn't mean that the way it came out. I just—"

"I'm not a shitty situation, you bastard." She glared at both men, turned, and ran for the bedroom.

Nausea rose in Ethan's throat. "Jesus Christ."

"You said she wasn't home!" Sebastian said, running a hand over his face, obviously upset.

"She wasn't supposed to be." But she looked like she'd been napping or maybe she wasn't feeling well. Shit. "Stay here," Ethan muttered and headed to the bedroom.

He walked through the open door but the bathroom door was closed, and as he turned the handle, he found it locked. "Sienna." He banged on the door. "Let me in."

"I'm sick. I'll be out in a few minutes."

He sat on the bed, waiting, pissed that the night had gone so wrong. His plan had been to have dinner with Sienna and his brother, take Sebastian to Ethan's apartment, and return to propose to Sienna.

Instead, his brother had opened his big mouth and Sienna definitely had gotten the wrong idea.

When she didn't come out, he rose to his feet, prepared to knock the door down if he had to, when Sienna swung it open wide and stepped out.

Her face was pale, her eyes glassy, her dark hair falling in waves around her shoulders. She'd been talking about changing back to blonde. He didn't care what color hair she had, he loved *her*.

"Are you sick?" he asked carefully, tiptoeing around his brother's fuckup.

"Yes. I left work early. I figured I'd come home, nap, and wake up to meet with Ashley. I slept through my alarm." She folded her arms across her chest, putting a clear barrier up between them.

"Why didn't you call me?"

"Because I don't report in to you and I figured you'd want time with your brother." She walked over to the bed and sat down, curling up on her side.

He ignored the snide first remark because she was obviously pissed and hurt and rightly so. He sat down beside her, placing his hand on her arm. "You misunderstood what you heard Sebastian say."

She raised her head up enough to ask, "Oh? So you didn't tell him you didn't want kids?"

"I felt that way… at the time. But you know my head wasn't on straight back then." And he really didn't think he needed to rehash his past with her when she knew it well already.

She swallowed hard. "Yet despite how good things have been these last few months, your brother thinks you're making the best of a *shit situation*," she said, affecting quotation marks with her hands.

"Because he doesn't know anything about us."

Her eyes opened wide and he realized he'd made a strategic error.

"You didn't think to tell him you were happy here? Is that because you were just pretending? Making the best of it? Of me?" Tears filled her eyes and it ripped him apart inside.

"Fuck no," he said, suddenly desperate for her to understand. "I expressed some of how I felt but not everything. You know I'm not an open, talkative person. I wasn't going to call Sebastian and gush over the fact that I fell in love with you!" he said, raising his voice.

"You what?" Her voice grew soft, her tone surprised.

He stood and fished the ring out of his pocket,

then knelt down beside the edge of the bed. "I fell in love with you, Sienna Dare. I wasn't prepared for you. You got under my skin, ripped away all my preconceived notions of what I wanted out of life, and I can't imagine living without you."

She ran her tongue over her lips. "Why didn't you say anything?" she asked, her voice trembling.

"Because I didn't want to make you choose between Miami and your life and family ... and me. And I think a part of me was petrified you'd turn me down."

She shook her head hard. "Never," she whispered.

"In case you're worried I feel pressured into this or stuck, you should know that I don't. I'm desperate to make you my wife."

He held out the ring he'd picked out, having called her mother and asked for a guesstimation of Sienna's ring size.

Once he decided to ask her, he wanted his ring on her finger the minute she said yes.

The three-carat emerald-cut stone with tiny individual halo diamonds surrounding it and covering the band glittered in his hand. "Sienna, will you marry me? Be my better half for the rest of my life? For better, for worse, in sickness and in health ... and in New York," he added for ultimate clarification.

She laughed, tears streaming from her eyes as she

said, "Yes! Yes, I'll marry you."

He slipped the ring onto her finger, pleased it fit and she could wear it from now on. Then he leaned in and pressed his mouth against hers, tasting the salt on her lips and drinking in her sweet essence.

"Knock knock." Sebastian walked into the room. "Sorry to interrupt but I couldn't stand it a second longer. I'm so damned sorry. I didn't know you were home when I spoke–"

"Why don't you quit while you're ahead," Sienna suggested, laughing and holding out her now ringed hand. "Especially since we're going to be related."

God, Ethan loved this woman and her easygoing approach to life. She rolled with the punches, something she'd need if she was going to be married to him. And have his kids.

"I want more than one kid," he heard himself say. Unplanned and taking him off guard.

She grinned. "Good because so do I."

"Does this mean I'm forgiven?" Sebastian asked.

"Yes," Sienna said.

"Now get the hell out." Ethan waved his brother away.

Taking the hint, Sebastian stepped out and pulled the door closed behind him.

✧　✧　✧

"MIND IF I get up?" Ethan asked from his kneeling position. "My knees are cramping." He rose and climbed into bed with her, pulling her into his arms. "I love you. I just wish I'd said it before and more often."

Sienna's heart beat with pure joy and happiness. "I'm just glad you're saying it now and will forever. That works for me because I love you too. So much."

Ethan loved her. He wanted her to come and live in New York with him. It was everything she'd ever wanted and never thought she'd have.

He slid her nightshirt up and, from behind, placed his palm against her belly. "I love you, Sienna," he said again. "You're giving me you. You're giving me a family. All things I never thought I'd have. Thank you, sweetheart."

He pressed his lips against her neck, his thick erection gliding along her back. She knew what he wanted but his brother was in the other room.

Good thing they had a lifetime to be together whenever they wanted.

Epilogue

*B*ABIES, BABIES, AND *more babies.*
Sienna held her baby girl in her arms.
Elizabeth.

Lizzy, named after Ethan's mother, was the perfect combination of both her parents, with a head of black hair like her daddy. Sienna had gone back to blonde and she had to admit the upkeep was a lot easier. And though Ethan had fallen in love with her with dark hair, he had a thing for her blonde locks. Her lower body was in no mood to think about his reaction the day he'd first seen her with lighter hair … but if she hadn't already been pregnant? Yeah, he'd have been potent that day.

She grinned at her sweet little baby.

And Ethan snapped another picture with his phone.

Sienna's family had flown to New York a few days after she'd given birth and they'd walked through her apartment one by one, each holding Lizzy, cooing at the baby, and to Sienna's pleasure, making nice with her husband.

Yep, her husband.

Sienna and Ethan had married in Miami, with the entire family present. All, that is, but Robert Dare, who had disappeared with his mistress. They thought he'd gone to Barbados, at least that's what his secretary had let slip, but nobody was sure. Nor did they care.

What made Sienna's wedding day even better? Her half siblings had finally embraced her mother. It was like their father's affair had solidified placing the blame for everything on his shoulders. Had Savannah made a mistake staying involved with Robert once she'd known he was married? Yes, but they were all ready to let past hurts go.

The Dare and Knight families had babies galore these days. Ethan's sister had had a little girl they named Jillian, Parker's wife, Emily, had a boy named Roscoe after her mother, Riley had her girl, Gracie, and now Ashley was pregnant. Added to the rest of the children and Christmas was going to be awesome next year.

"Can I put her into the bassinette?" Ethan asked, gazing down at his sleeping daughter, a look that had Sienna's heart melting and her falling in love with her husband all over again.

"Sure."

He carefully lifted his baby girl and placed her

down into the bassinette by the bed in their room. Then he slid in beside her.

"You did it." He pulled her into his arms.

"We did it. You got me to the hospital in time, after all."

He chuckled. "I'm not sure I could be happier," he said.

"Me neither. And you know that question you asked me? What do I want to do now that I'm living in New York?"

He nodded. "Any business you want, I can get you an interview. Any nonprofit would be lucky to have you."

She swallowed hard. "How about our kids? How would they feel about having a stay-at-home mom who ran charitable events when she could carve out the time?"

He pressed his lips to hers. "I think they'd love it. And as long as you're happy, I will be, too."

✧   ✧   ✧

ETHAN GLANCED AT his watch. If Sienna didn't hurry, they were going to be late. He debated on yelling for her, then decided against it. For one thing, he didn't want to wake the baby, and for another, he knew better than to rush a woman getting ready to go out for the evening. For the first time since having a baby.

A baby they were leaving with a sitter who came highly recommended but was a stranger they'd interviewed twice and called every reference she had.

Chances were they'd be home within the hour, but he and Sienna agreed they had to go to a happy hour event at her brother Jason's Club TEN29, the hottest New York City nightclub around. With the lack of sleep they'd endured lately, Ethan was glad this would be an early night.

Jason Dare, of all the brothers, was an enigma. He kept to himself, rarely went to family events, and was closest to the group of men he owned his club with. Men he called his *brothers*.

From Sienna, Ethan knew something had happened to Jason and those other men in college, an incident that had bonded them in a way few could understand. And though Sienna had shared the drama of that time, Ethan never brought it up with Jason. It wasn't something a person talked about like the weather; rather it defined the kind of man Jason had become.

He remembered asking Sienna the meaning behind the name of Club TEN29 and she'd replied, *it's the defining date in Jason's life.* Given what he now knew, the name was appropriate. A fitting memorial.

Ethan glanced at his watch again and groaned. "Sienna!" he called, knowing they had to leave or else they'd be late.

"I'm coming! I was just checking on the sitter and the baby." Mara, the babysitter, was sitting in the rocker with Lizzy in her arms.

Ethan knew it was going to be difficult for them to leave her. He looked up, his gaze lit on his wife, and his breath left his body in a whoosh, leaving him light-headed.

"Jesus, you're gorgeous."

"You like?" She stepped into the room wearing a strappy red dress that draped over one shoulder and slid over her body like a caress. The hem ended mid-thigh, revealing her long, sexy legs that were covered in a sandal with a red sole she made sure to show him. "See? I match."

He grinned, wrapping an arm around her and dipping her low. "Do you know what tonight is?" he asked.

"Six weeks," she whispered through bright red lips that also matched her outfit. Her long hair fell around her shoulders and he raised her to a standing position.

Six long weeks and his cock had felt every last second. "I'm going to bring you home after this damned event and fuck my wife," he whispered into her ear.

She shivered and her nipples puckered beneath the sheath of her dress.

"Are you not wearing a bra?" he asked on a low

growl.

"You'll find out later." She spun away. "Can we go? I want to get there, be seen, and come home so I can check on my baby … and then make love to my sexy husband."

If he had to put up with Jason Dare in order to make it back here for the main event, Ethan figured he could deal. Especially since he'd end the night buried deep inside the wife he adored.

Can't get enough Dares? **SEXY DARE** starring Jason Dare is up next.

SEXY DARE

He's sexy and brooding … She's sweetness and light.

Owning a nightclub has its advantages, and for alpha billionaire Jason Dare, the perks of enjoying a woman's company without any expectations works perfectly for him … until he rescues Faith Lancaster from the side of the road and is tempted by more than just her *sweet treats*.

Faith has spent the past year building her candy business, Sweet Treats, into a profitable company. Men and dating haven't been a priority, but she's never met anyone like Jason Dare, either. Sexy and irresistible, he awakens desires she didn't know existed and it doesn't take her long to succumb to his charms.

Both of them have their reasons for keeping things casual, but when someone from Faith's past starts threatening her future, will Jason finally decide to claim the woman meant to be his?

Photo: Wander Aguiar
Cover by Lori Jackson Design

Chapter One

W ITH HAPPY HOUR being celebrated loudly around him, Jason Dare stood on a balcony above the bar area and surveyed his domain, Club TEN29, a nightclub in Tribeca, an ode to the past and a reminder that the future wasn't guaranteed. Despite the fact that his two other partners were here, as were members of his actual family, he still felt very much alone.

Although solitary was a state of being he chose for reasons only he and his partners – men he considered his brothers – understood, sometimes it wasn't easy, especially since they were very much in demand. As owners, they were becoming well-known here and had had extremely positive press, and that made him a target – for those who wanted an in with the occasional high-brow guest, and women with dollar signs in their eyes and hopes to snag a wealthy man as their goal. Jason didn't engage. He was ultra-selective with the females he brought to his bed.

His life was the club, his partners and his large family. He kept his circle close and *minimized his risk of loss* as best he could. That mantra defined him, extending into his love life, as well. After his father had blown his family sky high, after he'd almost his sister to cancer when she was a child, after losing his partner, Landon's twin, and Jason's best friend, back in college, he didn't, couldn't get close to people and risk more loss.

He didn't get emotionally involved. Ever. A woman couldn't expect anything more than the occasional hookup when it was convenient but he enjoyed those moments of connection with the females he did allow into his bed. He had enough darkness in his life that when he let go, he wanted to enjoy and have fun.

"Jason, this has been an amazing night!" his sister, Sienna, said, throwing her arms around his neck and planting a kiss on his cheek.

He chuckled and smiled at her glowing face.

Her husband, Ethan Knight, grinned as he pulled her off him and into his arms. "She's been liberal with the alcohol." Ethan explained her exuberant enthusiasm. "Her first time out since having the baby." He held his wife tight against him.

"I had fun! And now we're going home to F–" Ethan placed a hand over Sienna's mouth, sparing Jason from hearing about his sister's love life. Jesus.

He shot the man a grateful look.

"And on that note, we're leaving. We just wanted to say goodbye," Ethan said with a smug grin on his face.

"Thanks for coming." Jason extended his arm and shook Ethan's hand. "And give that little bundle a kiss from her Uncle Jase."

Accepting this man as his sister's husband had been an adjustment, one Jason was still making, considering Ethan had knocked up Sienna before anyone even knew they were together. They now had a baby girl named Lizzy who Jason adored, and Ethan was a member of the family. More people for Jason to worry about. He watched them leave, acknowledging his sister was in good hands with the other man.

His gaze turned to his closest friends since their time together in college, now equal partners in Club TEN29. They stood huddled together around the bar with some of their repeat customers. Tanner Grayson was the Night Manager, and Landon Bennett was the head of Entertainment and Appearances, Brand Deals and Promotions. After Landon's twin died, he'd pulled into himself, while Tanner had spiraled, and it was only by sheer determination that he'd dragged himself out of the angry place to which he'd gone and the trouble in which he'd gotten himself into.

Jason held the position of CEO. Together they were a solid mix of personalities and work ethic in a club that was merely two years old but becoming prominent in the club scene. They made sure Club TEN29 provided a memorable experience for everyone who stepped inside. There was no task too menial they wouldn't handle personally if the need arose.

But Jason wanted *more* for their singular club. They had a stage on which customers danced but it wasn't fully utilized, and although they'd put a lot of money into ads and promotions, they weren't growing as fast as he would like. He just hadn't figured out in which direction they needed to go in order to break out the way he wanted. Since Tanner and Landon thought things were fine as they were, Jason needed a fully fleshed out plan before presenting it to them for a vote. Which was why he was meeting his cousin Gabe later on tonight. To hash out some ideas.

Gabriel Dare owned Elite, a nightclub that operated on a scale Jason couldn't imagine, one where people paid over five figures for a table and A-list celebrities visited often. They had clubs all over the world, including on the island of Eden, an exclusive, invitation only resort near the Bermuda Triangle.

He also wanted to pull Gabe in on an issue they were having with another club owner who had begun sabotaging their business. Clearly their success threatened Daniel Sutherland, the owner of Club Rocket, a nearby nightclub. After a series of glitches in software and music that couldn't be accidental, last night someone had smashed windows of cars in the lot where Club TEN29 customers parked.

The night employee had *miraculously* been on a bathroom break when the incident occurred but a customer had run back to the club and informed security. The three partners had accompanied their guard to the lot and found one of the kids with a bat in hand sneaking out. In exchange for not reporting him, they'd discovered a group had been paid well by Club Rocket's owner to destroy the cars and make people fear for their safety and that of their vehicles at the Club. Gabe had been through a similar issue, so Jason wanted his input.

He wanted to think things through before he met up with Gabe and he couldn't make decisions here, where the music blared and people partied. As much as Club TEN29 was home, Jason needed a break.

After clearing his departure with Tanner and Landon, Jason headed out into the cold air. He pulled his wool jacket around him and headed to his car. Despite it being impractical in the city, he liked having his Jag at his disposal.

Once he was enclosed in the luxurious interior and the heated seats and warmth began to surround him, he relaxed. He turned on some music and decided to drive around a little before heading to his cousin's. This area of the city wasn't the grid of ease that was uptown Manhattan and he wound his way through the smaller streets, taking in the shops that lined them.

Because it was cold, not many people were out so when he came upon a lone van parked in front of a rundown apartment building, with two women standing alongside it, he slowed down. When one of the women bent over, her cute ass peeking out from beneath the edge of her down jacket, he noticed. And when she kicked what he realized was a flat tire in frustration, he came to a complete stop, then parked his car in front of hers.

As he climbed out and got a look at the curvy woman with waves of blonde hair, full lips and a startled expression on her pretty face, currently clutching the lug wrench in her hand like a weapon, he realized his night was about to get much more exciting.

✧ ✧ ✧

FAITH LANCASTER LOADED the last of her marshmallow pops into the back of her company van, adjusting the baskets, taking care to space the items far enough apart that nothing would get ruined or crushed. She'd spent all day in her small apartment kitchen, making and wrapping her treats with the intention of dropping off baskets to nearby stores along with her business cards. She planned to request they leave them on the counter for their customers to sample, hoping to drive business to Sweet Treats, her candy store located off the beaten path.

Kelsey Johnson, the culinary school intern Faith had hired to help, joined her after working in the shop all day. Before she and Faith could climb into the car, Faith noticed her flat back tire and groaned.

The deflated tire mocked her and all the time she'd spent creating and preparing. Although she could have handed them out during the day, she'd ended up spending all afternoon cooking and creating, deciding to work from home instead of the shop, and now it was early evening. But she knew the area she wanted to hit up had open stores with people browsing for the evening. A used bookstore, a coffee shop, and a few other boutique type stores that would hopefully help out a fellow business.

She should have known better than to drop a big chunk of change on an old beat up delivery van with no known history but desperation made a woman do stupid things. And Faith, although she'd come a long way, had been desperate when she'd arrived in Manhattan with a new name, a limited amount of funds and a dream of opening her own candy shop.

She glared at the flat on the back tire, wondering why luck just wasn't on her side. She'd had a rough go of it for a long time now and she'd thought she was coming out on the other side at last. Now this.

"Kelsey, can you grab the wrench in the back? Just be careful not to knock over the candy. I'll deal with checking out the spare once I see if I can even get the lug nuts off." Assuming this old van even had a spare.

Kelsey, a pretty girl with brown hair and bangs, met Faith's gaze, eyes wide. "You can change a tire?" the twenty one year old asked.

Faith managed a laugh or else she might cry in frustration. "I'm going to try."

When Faith was young, her dad, before abandoning Faith and her mother and older brother, had been a car fanatic. *Always have a lug wrench in your car, baby girl. It'll save you any time you have a flat.* Not that a ten year old knew anything about changing tires but Faith had hung on her daddy's every word until one day he hadn't come home. After that, Faith had given up on learning about cars but she knew what she had to do from a class she'd taken in high school.

Accepting the long iron from Kelsey, she knelt

down by the tire once more. When all her strength wouldn't turn the nut and she tried all four of them, she groaned, rose to her feet and kicked at the tire in annoyance.

"Pretty sure that won't help," Kelsey said, just as Faith muttered an obscene curse thanks to the pain shooting through her foot.

She was in so much agony, she barely registered the car stopping then pulling into the open spot in front of her van until a large man approached them, making her aware they were two women alone on an empty street in the dark.

Using the wrench as her defense, she held it up in front of her. "Don't come near us."

"Relax." He stepped to the side until he was underneath a street lamp, the glow illuminating his features. "Do I look like a killer to you?"

She studied him, a handsome man with dark brown hair, in a wool coat with his tie visible. "Ted Bundy was handsome, too."

He grinned and her heart skipped a beat. My God, he was good looking. A dimple beside that amazing smile winked at her and body parts she'd thought long dead came to life.

"Thank you … I think?" He said with a shake of his head. "Or not. Look, you obviously need help." He strode past her, ignoring her weaponry and knelt down by the tire. "What about roadside assistance? Did you call?"

She glanced at his obviously expensive coat, had noted his suit beneath and brand name shoes. "Umm, does this old hunk of junk look like it comes with roadside assistance?" She shot him a look of disbelief. "Some of us can't afford luxuries and AAA is definitely a luxury."

From somewhere behind her, Kelsey, who had been silent, laughed out loud.

When he didn't immediately reply, Faith braced her hands on her hips and studied him, wondering why he'd stopped in the first place. "Listen, I appreciate the fact that you tried to help but I'll figure something out."

He slowly rose to his feet. "Do you have a spare? You must if you were trying to take this one off."

"I assume I do, underneath all the baskets I just loaded into the back." She heard the frustration in her voice and fought back an inkling of defeat. She wasn't going to fall apart over a flat tire and ruined plans.

"You assume?" He shook his head and strode around to the back end of the van, glancing inside and muttering a curse.

"There's no obvious spare in here, so we'll have to unload all this to see what's underneath. What is all that anyway?" he asked.

"Candy. Home made."

"Interesting." He raised his eyebrows, his gaze going from the sweet treats in the back to her face before he spoke. "Jason Dare," he said, extending his hand.

"Faith Lancaster." She placed her hand in his and the heat of his skin sizzled against her palm.

"Nice to meet you, Faith." He curled his fingers around hers and lingered longer than was necessary for a handshake. Long enough for her body to tingle with awareness before he released her.

"And this is my intern, Kelsey," Faith said.

The other woman smiled at him but didn't shake his hand.

"What do you do for a living?" Faith asked in a husky voice she barely recognized, her entire body still hyper aware of that one brush of his skin.

"I own a nightclub. Club TEN29. Have you heard of it?" he asked.

She shook her head. She never went out to party at night so what would she know about the club scene? But this man looked like he fit into it, with his sexy tousled brown hair that he probably paid a fortune to get cut so it fell just that way.

"Oh my God! My friends and I have been dying to go but there's always such a long line to get in," Kelsey said, her excitement tangible.

She'd been so quiet, Faith had almost forgotten

she was there.

"Well here's my business card," Jason said, putting his hand in his coat pocket and coming out with a few cards. He handed one to Kelsey, who was bouncing on her feet in excitement. "Just show it to security and they'll let you right in or at the very least call me."

"Oh my God, thank you!" she practically squealed.

His gaze settled on Faith's face. "Now, let's see to that spare."

✧   ✧   ✧

IF JASON HAD to peg the type of woman he liked, tall and willowy would describe most of his hook-ups, yet he couldn't stop staring at the full-figured, curvy blonde with the porcelain skin and full lips who created candy, of all things.

"Let's move the baskets back to the apartment," Faith said, breaking the spell that had woven between them as they stared at one another, both clearly struck by something bigger than them both.

"I'll take some." Kelsey walked between them and started to work.

Together they unloaded the candy, which Faith and her assistant brought back upstairs to what he assumed was her apartment while he did something he hadn't done since college.

It was a miracle he knew how to change a tire.

For sure, his father, Robert Dare, hadn't taught him as he'd rarely been around. Maybe he'd taught Jason's half-brothers from a woman nobody knew about to handle the things a man should know. Shaking off that painful memory, Jason called his cousin Gabe and let him know he would be late, before throwing his jacket into the back of his car, rolling up his sleeves, loosening his tie and getting down to his task.

While he worked, Kelsey called an Uber to take her home and one showed up quickly. Apparently Faith, having taken one of his business cards, had decided he was a legitimate businessman and safe to be alone with.

It didn't take long to get the tire off the car and on examination, Jason realized it had been deliberately slashed and that bothered him.

"How's it going?" Faith asked him.

"No problems, unless you count the fact that someone deliberately cut your tire." He glanced over his shoulder.

Faith had frozen in place, her eyes wide, her concerned expression clearly telling him she was upset.

"It's probably some of the kids in the neighborhood," she finally said, visibly forcing herself to relax. "They congregate around here late at night and I haven't looked at the van since the day before yesterday."

He wasn't sure whether or not he believed her and he tucked her reaction away to dissect another time.

She wrapped her arms around herself, for the first time since he'd met her, appearing uncertain. And a fierce feeling of protectiveness rushed over him, one he'd previously experienced only for people he cared about, yet he didn't know this woman at all.

"So what are you doing with all the candy?" he asked as he worked on the tire, eager take that stricken look off her face, change the subject, shake off the weird emotions she provoked in him, and maybe get to know her, at the same time.

"I own a store called Sweet Treats," she said. "I want to build my business so I made baskets of my signature item and I was going to go around to the local businesses and ask if they'd put the candy and my business card by the register."

"What makes your candy stand out?" he asked.

"Other than how good it is?" she asked cheekily. "It's handcrafted and made with love. If I grow enough I'll have to bring in outside made candy to fill the cases but that's for another time. Meanwhile, I know I'm a small shop and it'll be hard to get my name out there but if I can dominate the area around my store based on the one thing I offer that's different than anyone else, then maybe word of mouth will work in my favor."

He listened to her words and his hand stilled on the last lug nut. Everything she said made sense.

Her words, *dominating the area and standing out* jumped out at him. "That's it!" he said excitement filling him because her words had hit on the one thing missing from Club TEN29. Something unique to them and suddenly he knew just what he needed to discuss with Gabe.

"What's it?" she asked.

"You've come up with a brilliant idea, Faith Lancaster. And it just might help me with my business, so thank you." He turned the wrench one last time and rose to his feet, his legs stiff from crouching in one position for so long.

"Happy to help." She shrugged, obviously confused but that was okay because he wasn't. He finally had direction.

He looked down at his hands, now completely covered in dirt and grease.

Faith glanced at his blackened skin. "Oh! Come upstairs and wash up. It's the least I can do for you after you saved me."

He didn't want to get into his car covered in filth and she seemed okay with him now so he nodded. "I'd appreciate that."

He followed her inside and up two flights of dark

stairs. He immediately didn't like where she lived, from the description of the guys hanging out front late at night to the lack of lighting in the walk up, it screamed danger. But who was he to judge? Yet it bothered him. He wouldn't let his sister live here.

By the time they walked into the small apartment, he was frowning but one look at the cheerful décor and his mood lightened. This was a woman who made the best of any situation, he realized, taking in the white curtains and the old furniture with bright pink throw pillows covering the cushions. A matching fun pink rug sat under a beat up coffee table, covered in well-read books.

"You like pink," he mused, coming up beside her. "And candy." She even smelled sweet and delicious. "Are you fun, Faith?"

Her cheeks turned an adorable shade of … pink. "I can be, in the right situation."

He wondered what that right situation might be because he'd definitely like to have fun with her. The kind between the sheets. Before his dick could react to that thought he asked, "Where's the bathroom?"

She led him to a small partly open door and gestured for him to go inside. "There's a tiny linen closet behind the door. Take a towel and get yourself cleaned up."

She stepped away and headed back to the main

area of the apartment.

He glanced over to where the small kitchen was visible through a pass-through. The candies were neatly stacked on the Formica countertops.

"So about those treats. Did I earn myself one?" he asked, joining her.

She blinked in surprise. "Why didn't I think of that?" She rushed to the kitchen, returning with a pop and handing it to him.

He bit into it once, then twice, quickly swallowing the sweet, delicious candy. "Mmm. Damn, these are good. S'mores flavor?" he asked.

She nodded, a grin on her face. "It's like a taste of home," she said softly.

Sensing this meant something to her, he wanted to know more. "How so?"

She sighed. "My mom and I used to make candy all the time when I was growing up. She always wanted to open a store in our small town but she didn't have the ability. Things were … out of her control. And she needed to work to take care of me and my brother. But this was her favorite recipe and it reminds me of her."

"What happened?" he asked. "If you want to talk about it."

"She died recently." Faith blinked and looked away.

Recognizing raw pain, he changed the subject. "Well, your candy is delicious and I hope you succeed," he said, treating her to a warm smile, realizing their time together was coming to an end.

"I have a meeting I need to get to," he said. But he wasn't ready to leave.

"Oh right." She rushed over to the kitchen and returned with a basket in her hand. "Take this. As a thank you. You're a good Samaritan, Jason Dare."

He accepted her gift, their hands brushing as it exchanged hands. A shot of electricity jolted up his arm and went straight to his cock. Something about this woman got to him, from her gorgeous face and curvaceous body to her strength and the hint of occasional fragility beneath. He knew with everything in him he ought to stay away. From the fact that her tire might have been slashed to the fact that she didn't radiate one night stand type of woman to him, he should say goodbye and walk out the door.

"Have dinner with me." He blurted out the words before he could think them through.

She stared at him in surprise, those pretty lips pursing in thought, green eyes huge. "Umm … I really don't think it's a good idea. I have too much going on right now and I don't date and … well, we shouldn't." She sounded sad, as if she didn't want to say no.

He rolled his shoulders, deciding it was for the best

even if he didn't like being turned down by her. "I understand."

She stared at him for a heartbeat. "Well, thanks again."

He inclined his head. "You can thank me by locking your door and being careful out there." Her slashed tire stayed with him, bothered him, even.

Sure, this was New York City and not the best neighborhood, so it really could have been done by someone who considered vandalism a good time. He'd probably have gone with that theory, too, if not for her slightly panicked reaction she'd tried to hide.

"Don't worry. I'm a big girl and I can take care of myself," she said, striding towards the door. "But I'll take your advice."

He stepped out the door she'd opened for him. "Bye sweetness," he said. "It was nice meeting you, Faith Lancaster."

She wrinkled her nose at the nickname.

"Would you prefer candy girl?" he asked, chuckling at the blush on her cheeks as he walked away.

IF FAITH DATED anyone, she would date Jason Dare. She leaned back against the door and sighed like a teenage girl crushing on her first date. My God, that man had an ass to die for.

When she hadn't been carrying candy baskets up-stairs she'd been ogling his rear end in his suit trousers. She could only imagine him naked and that was the idea that had her shivering when her thoughts should be on whether her slashed tire was a freak incident as she'd told Jason or a warning sign from the brother she ran away from.

When they were younger, she'd loved her brother but as he grew up, Colton developed... issues and that was putting it mildly. Drugs took over his life.

She stepped away from the door, hating that she was going down this train of thought but she couldn't help it. The tire had brought up all sorts of fears. And memories.

Colton showing up after her mom died unexpect-edly, demanding his share of the estate, only to find out he'd been disinherited. His rage and anger. Though her mom hadn't been wealthy, she wasn't poor. She'd had money from her parents which she'd saved, and she'd taken out a life insurance policy with Faith as the beneficiary.

She double checked the lock and deadbolt on her door, as the memories continued to flow. As much as Faith would have liked to share the money with her sibling, Faith agreed with her mom. Colton would throw the money away on drugs, so she honored her mother's wishes and refused him.

She should have known that wouldn't be the end of it. Colton came by high one night, broke into her apartment, grabbed her around the neck and threatened to kill her. That was the moment she understood the brother she'd known was lost to her and fear like she'd never known, encompassed her.

Maybe she should have called the police but she'd been more afraid of angering him more. She knew from experience he never stayed behind bars for long, no matter what petty crime they picked him up for. So within three days of his threats, she'd quit her job, packed up the necessities, and left her small midwestern town, heading to the biggest city she could think of where she could get lost.

She'd checked into hotel with cash, then found a lawyer willing to see her that same week and he filed paperwork to change her name from Faith Holland to Faith Lancaster. Understanding the rush, he'd pulled strings to get her in to see a judge, who he convinced her life was in danger. And as she still had faint bruises on her neck, and photographs she'd taken immediately after, he'd been willing to seal her records.

She'd been in New York for six months and she'd moved fast with everything she'd done. She had a new name, a new life, a shop she'd leased because it already had a commercial kitchen … and as she glanced around her apartment and out the window, she remembered she also had a slashed tire that may or may not present a problem.

Was it any wonder she'd turned Jason down? From the time her dad had left, leaving her to feel like it was her fault, that she was too much of a burden for him, she'd learned to distrust men. If the one who was supposed to love and take care of her couldn't stick around, why would someone she merely dated?

She wasn't a virgin but she definitely didn't get involved with many guys. Yet for the first time, she'd been severely tempted to break her no-dating rule. Jason got her blood pumping, desire flowing and he made her want to step out of the hidden comfort zone she'd cushioned herself in for most of her life.

But she couldn't. She knew better than to trust any guy, let alone a nightclub owner she'd just met. Even if he had been her savior tonight.

Want even more Carly books?
CARLY'S BOOKLIST by Series – visit:
http://smarturl.it/CarlyBooklist

Sign up for Carly's Newsletter:
http://smarturl.it/carlynews

Carly on Facebook:
facebook.com/CarlyPhillipsFanPage

Carly on Instagram:
instagram.com/carlyphillips

About the Author

Carly Phillips is the *N.Y. Times* and *USA Today* Best-selling Author of over 50 sexy contemporary romance novels featuring hot men, strong women and the emotionally compelling stories her readers have come to expect and love. Carly's career spans over a decade and a half with various New York publishing houses, and she is now an Indie author who runs her own business and loves every exciting minute of her publishing journey. Carly is happily married to her college sweetheart, the mother of two nearly adult daughters and three crazy dogs (two wheaten terriers and one mutant Havanese) who star on her Facebook Fan Page and website. Carly loves social media and is always around to interact with her readers. You can find out more about Carly at www.carlyphillips.com.

Made in the USA
Middletown, DE
02 August 2019